# THE BARBARIAN BEFORE CHRISTMAS

AN ICE PLANET BARBARIANS NOVELLA

RUBY DIXON

RUBY DIXON

Photograph by Sara Eirew Photographer

Cover Design by Kati Wilde

❀ Created with Vellum

# THE BARBARIAN BEFORE CHRISTMAS

The growing barbarian tribe is about to celebrate No-Poison Day – a time of love, laughter, and gifts. But all Elly wants is for her mate to be at her side before the brutal season arrives. All Bek wants is a way to quickly return to his female despite the mountains between them. Thanks to the talents of a newcomer...they're both about to get their wish and celebrate the happiest of holidays together.

This novella features characters from prior Ice Planet Barbarians stories and DOES NOT stand alone.

# AUTHOR'S NOTE

This story falls a little bit after the end of Icehome #1 (Lauren's Barbarian). If you've been reading along and are all caught up, great! You'll remember who all these people are.

If you're behind a few books and just want to read about our blue boys, there are a few newcomers from another slave ship on the far side of the mountains, and Vektal and a lot of the hunters from the main tribe have been away from home helping them get set up to survive. There! Now you're all caught up. :)

Veronica and Ashtar are mentioned a lot in this particular book, but if you've read my dragon series, there's no surprise as to what Ashtar is. You haven't missed their book. It's coming up. I just really wanted to write this story now instead of a few months from now. We'll circle back to them. I promise.

And a tiny housekeeping note. I try to keep tabs on everyone that moves back and forth between tribes and ages and so on and so forth. That being said, I've caught myself in a mistake. In LAUREN'S BARBARIAN and BARBARIAN'S TEASE, the list of hunters that go with Vektal does not include Aehako. I'm not entirely sure why, because in my head, he's always been there. I wrote this entire story and then realized too late when I cross-referenced my notes that he wasn't in the list of hunters mentioned there. So I could either scrap the scenes I've written for them in this book, or admit my goof.

I love what I've written too much, so mea culpa! Please ignore my mistake and pretend like he was there the entire time, just hanging in the shadows. It didn't affect either one of those stories in any way, shape or form, so I feel comfortable "inserting" him into the storyline.

With all that out of the way...enjoy!

<3 Ruby

# 1

BEK

I scan the sandy shore, as I do every morning, looking for pretty things. Yesterday there was a rock in the shape of a swirling circle, and the day before, a strange dried creature that looked like a giant pinkish burr. This day, there is nothing of particular interest, and it makes my mood even more sour than usual.

At least if I could find a gift for my Ell-ee, this day would not be a waste. Instead, every day here on the shore, coddling the newcomers, is a day I do not spend with my mate. It is she who should be getting all my attention, not these new tribesmates who scream at the sight of a fresh kill or cringe when something needs to be gutted. At least the strangers from the island are not as bad as the humans, but I have no patience for those that keep me from my mate. Any patience I had disappeared many nights ago.

I kick at the sand with my boot and uncover a large crystalline granule that looks as if it has a hole punched through it. I squat to pick it up, my tail flicking against the rocky shore, and examine it. This could be a necklace, I think. I can braid a decorative cord delicate enough for my Ell-ee's neck, and I imagine placing it against her skin, the warmth and trust in her eyes as she gazes up at me...and I bite back a groan of frustration and anger.

To think that I have spent so long away from my mate, after so many seasons without her. This cannot be borne. I should be at her side, pampering her. Making her feel safe. We have been gone for a full turn of the moons now, and I miss her as if my heart is gone from my chest. More than that, I worry about her. My Ell-ee is brave, but she is fragile in her own way. Who will be there to hold her when she has bad dreams? Who will be there to take a bite of her food so she knows it is safe to eat? She needs me and I...I need her just as badly. It feels as if I am half alive without her.

With a snarl, I straighten and kick the sand.

"Ho," calls Rokan, approaching from behind me. "You stomp like a kit deprived of his favorite toy. What troubles you this day?"

"Do you not know?" I snap at him, irritated. "You are the one that can sense things that cannot be seen. You tell me what troubles me."

He moves to stand next to me and leans on his spear heavily, gazing out into the rolling, endless waters of the great salt lake. "The same thing that troubles me. I miss my mate. I need to be at her side."

I grunt, because as always, he is not wrong. "And yet we are trapped here. Looking after those with less skill than a kit, hand-feeding them and coddling them."

"That is unfair," Rokan chides me. "The human females are new to this world entirely, and those from the island are not used to this cold. They will learn quickly. Already they work hard and need us less every day."

What he says is true, but I cannot bring myself to feel anything less than annoyed at them. I flip the smooth crystal in my hand, thoughtful. "We have not been mates for very long. It is...difficult to leave her."

"It does not grow easier," Rokan tells me. "My Li-lah is about to give birth to our kit soon, and I think of her constantly. Her and my little Rollan. I hoped to be home before they celebrate No-Poison Day. Rollan loves it so much. It is a joy to watch his face when the decorations are hung."

Ah yes. The human celebration in which they decorate a puny tree and wish for showers of plants that are not poisonous to show that they are loved. It is a bizarre thing to celebrate, but the humans have many odd habits. I think of the small gifts I have been acquiring for my Ell-ee every day. I have many pretty shells for her, odd trinkets, and a large bag of salt to flavor food. I think of the No-Poison Day and wonder if my Ell-ee would enjoy it. I like the thought of showering her with plants so she will give me kisses. I want to make her feel as special as the other human females do. No, even more so, because she is mine. "No-Poison Day will be very soon now," I say, and my tone is surly. "It is yet another thing we miss out on."

"I do not think so," Rokan says, gazing out at the water again before turning to me. "I must return. You and Aehako as well. We are needed."

My heart seizes in my chest. I clench his arm, terrified. "What have you seen?"

"Nothing bad," he reassures me, prying my bruising grip off of his bicep. "Just that you are needed at home. It is a feeling I have.

And I feel my Li-lah needs me at home, as well. I think our new kit will be coming very soon. I plan on speaking to Vektal about this. Will you join me?"

I nod. It would take being swallowed by a sky-claw to keep me from this. Even if Vektal says no, I will venture home anyhow. If my Ell-ee needs me, I must be there.

MOST OF THE newcomers are busy crafting huts along the distant cliff so that all of the island's tribes can be housed warmly. It is a task that has consumed many days, but there is much laughter and joy from them as they work. It just reminds me that we are not needed here as badly as we are at home, and I am all the more convinced that I should return to my Ell-ee.

We find the chief sitting with two of the newcomers, the golden male called Ash-tar and his female, the human Vuh-ron-ca. They gesture that we should join them near the fire on the beach. I sit down, and Rokan immediately leaves. "A moment," he says, and then I am left staring at the others. They look at me expectantly.

I cannot help but scowl. Rokan has a smoother tongue than I do. He should be the one talking, yet here I am alone. I consider for a moment, and then say, "I wish to return home to my mate.".

"You think I do not?" Vektal's tone is even and full of humor. "It has been far too long since I have laid eyes upon my Georgie and my daughters."

"Not all of us are needed," I continue, when Ash-tar and Vuh-ron-ca remain silent. "Some of us can start the journey home. We have been here too long already. These others can join us at the village," I say with a flick of my wrist to indicate the newcomers, "Or they can stay here to survive, but I will not remain."

Vektal's mouth flattens with displeasure at my tone. It sounds very much as if I am challenging him, but I cannot hold back. My need for my Ell-ee is too great. But Rokan returns a moment later, with a sweaty Aehako at his side, and they thump down by the fire next to me.

"Now we are all here," Rokan says. "So we can discuss our journey."

I notice Ash-tar puts a hand on Vuh-ron-ca's thigh, gazing out at us with a calm expression. His eyes seem to change color, which is odd to me, but there are many odd things about these newcomers. She puts her hand over his and clears her throat. "We were actually just talking with Vektal about traveling to the village. I wish to study with Maylak, learn more about healing."

My sister? Eh? I have forgotten that Vuh-ron-ca has a healer's gift as well. Excitement flares in my chest and I look back to my chief. "There is talk of a journey, then?"

"There was, before you came and sat with your demands," he tells me. "Eventually all will be returning. A few will stay—I have talked to Farli and Mardok, and they will stay for now to help the others. So will Buh-brukh and Taushen, since they are newly resonated and do not need to worry about a kit for now."

"The females Leezh and Har-loh are very pregnant. They will not wish to make the long journey back on foot, either," I suggest. If others will stay then that means I can go.

Vuh-ron-ca and Ash-tar exchange a look. "It doesn't exactly have to be on foot," the human female says slowly, and twines her fingers with her mate's. I notice they have the same number of fingers—unlike the sa-khui, who have four fingers to the human five—but his are larger and claw-tipped and far more dangerous. She continues, "There's another way."

"I do not mind staying, if I must," Aehako says, speaking up for the first time. "I miss my mate and my little Kae fiercely, but they will understand if others must remain. These hunters from the island are good at many things, but have you seen one of them get caught in a snow drift? It is the most amusing—"

"No, you must go with us," Rokan says, interrupting. "You are needed back at home."

Aehako goes still, and the friendly, open expression on his face disappears. "What have you seen?"

"I have seen nothing bad," Rokan continues. "But I know that you are needed at home, as is Bek."

Aehako exchanges a look with me, and his smile is gone. His jaw clenches and he rubs a hand along it for a moment, then says, "I can be ready to leave before the suns get high in the sky."

I grunt agreement. He is like me—nothing comes before a mate. Nothing.

“Let us not go to extremes,” Vektal interrupts, raising a hand. “Rokan says it is nothing bad and he would know. There is no need to race out unprepared. The others that cannot go back will wish to send things along for family. I have already spoken with Leezh and Raahosh, and they are disappointed they cannot return yet, but they will stay for now and send gifts back for their girls. We will need food and supplies, and we will need a sad-full.”

Vuh-ron-ca clears her throat delicately. “Um. Saddle. A big one. Actually, Ashtar and I already have something in mind. We can be ready to go in the morning.”

I scowl at them, because a human female—especially this one, who is clumsy and weak—will only slow us down. “We do not need you to come with us. We will go faster without you.”

Ash-tar bares his fangs at me, his eyes growing dark. Vuh-ron-ca squeezes his hand and gives me a funny look. "How do you think you're going to get there without us? You need Ashtar, and he won't go without me."

"Bah. We do not need either of you."

"We do if we wish to get there in a much shorter period of time," Vektal corrects. He frowns at me as if I am making things worse with my protests. I do not care—all I can think about is my mate and how she has been alone all these long nights.

"I do not understand," Aehako says slowly, leaning forward. "Do you two know of a secret path?"

The mated pair exchange a glance. "Something along those lines," Vuh-ron-ca says. Vektal rubs his jaw and smirks, glancing over at me.

I do not trust this. Something is afoot. And yet... "How much quicker?" I ask, because this has my interest.

Vuh-ron-ca looks to her mate. Ash-tar thinks for a moment, and then says, "We can be over the mountains in a matter of hours. To your home in a day or so, provided the weather is clear."

A day? I could be holding my Ell-ee by this time tomorrow night? "Whatever it is, I will do it," I say quickly, before anyone can change their minds.

"I thought this might be so," my chief says in a dry voice. "How many can you carry, Ash-tar?"

The golden male does not hesitate. "Four, along with my mate. We can judge future trips based off of this one."

"Hold a moment...carry?" I sputter. I must misunderstand, because this makes no sense to me. The golden male wishes to carry us across the mountains?

"Carry," Ash-tar agrees, and there is a smug look on his fanged face.

I am speechless...but it does not matter, because I am going home to my mate. If he said I must carry him on my back through the churning salt waters, I would, as long as Ell-ee would be waiting for me on the other side.

# 2

**ELLY**

The stars aren't the same without Bek here at my side. Alone, they seem less bright, less welcoming. Then again, everything does. All the things that I took great joy in a few short weeks ago seem unable to bring me happiness anymore. Clear, starry nights are unexciting. Sunny, windy days hold no joy. The warmth of hot tea or the laughter of friends mean nothing. I thought that after I was free from cages and slavery that nothing in the world would bother me ever again...but I was wrong.

I miss Bek. I miss him so much that I hurt. I miss him so intensely that I want to just crawl into my furs and sleep and sleep and sleep until he returns. I know this isn't healthy. I know that I should be strong and independent and spend my time helping out the others, like Gail and Stacy and Claire and all the other tribeswomen. Bek loves me. He is going to return. He promised.

But the waiting is so, so hard. Lately it seems harder than ever, because my stomach has been growing increasingly upset, and I want fresh, raw meat…but Bek is not here to take a bite of my food and make it safe for me. He is not here to wrap his body around my cold one at night and keep me warm, and I do not trust the others enough to share heat. I am not good at being alone. Not anymore. Not when I had a glimpse of what life is like as his mate.

I close my eyes and huddle in my blankets, dreaming of him. His proud, stern face. The smooth arch of his tall horns and the long, dark braids he ties back along his temples to keep his hair out of his eyes. I think of the way he feels when he nuzzles me early in the morning, his velvet-soft skin brushing against mine, his tail tickling along my thigh. He holds me so tenderly and caresses me, murmuring a morning greeting before kissing every inch of my skin and showing how much he missed me while he was asleep. My throat knots up just thinking about it and hot tears seep out between my lashes and crust into ice. I rub it away with my fingers.

I don't even mind the cold when he's here. When he's not…well, I mind everything.

"Ell-ee," a little voice bellows outside my hut. A small hand scratches at the privacy screen. "Wake up! It's time to go catch dirtbeaks!"

Erevair. I haven't forgotten about our little morning "date." It's just that some mornings it's harder to crawl out of bed than others.

I pull myself from the blankets and put on my boots, then push my hair out of my face and go to the screen, pulling it back so my young visitor can enter.

"About time," Erevair declares as he enters, and he sounds just like Claire. Behind him trails a little girl with a long, silky brown braid and pale blue skin. It's Kae, Kira and Aehako's daughter, and she's as quiet as Erevair is noisy. "Have you eaten today, Elly?" Erevair moves next to my firepit and stirs the coals with my fire-stick. "It's too cold in here. Bek wouldn't like that."

Kae squats next to Erevair, content to watch him putter around my house as if it's his place. It's rather amusing to watch him. It's like he's trying to make up for the fact that Bek is gone by taking care of me. It's sweet, really.

"I ate," I lie. I'm low on my rations that Bek has already "tasted" for me and I'm saving them. I can skip a few meals.

"You're getting too skinny," Erevair says. "Bek won't like that." He pulls out a pouch of cakes, takes a bite of one like he's seen Bek do, and then offers it to me.

I can't help but smile. Even though he's a child, he's taken on quite a few of Bek's mannerisms, and he must have noticed that I only eat after Bek's tasted something. I eat the cake while he stirs my fire again, and then grabs a set of fur wraps, handing them to me when I finish my food. "We've got lots to do today. Kae's mama wants us to get her some eggs, and my mama wants more nests. And then she said I have to wash my hands."

Wise mama. The dirtbeaks make their nests from dvisti poop, so I don't blame Claire for demanding a hand-washing. I get to my feet and put on my wraps, and then offer the children my hand. "Let's go."

Erevair takes Kae's little hand in his and links his tail with hers, then puts his hand in mine so we form a chain. We do this every morning, though it's not always Kae that's with us. Sometimes it's Rukhar, or Liz or Georgie's girls. But I think Kae is his favorite. She's very quiet, which gives him a lot of room to talk. Joden,

Josie's oldest, came with us once and Erevair spent the entire time trying to talk over him. It was exhausting.

As we emerge from my hut, I see Kira sitting in front of hers, chatting with Claire. They have their sewing out and wave as they see us. For some reason the children love gathering dirtbeak nests, so I always have company with this particular chore. My gathering basket leans against the wall of the hut and I shake the snow off of it, then tuck it under my free arm. "Egg basket?" I ask in a low voice, and Kae detangles herself from Erevair and trots over to her mother.

We wait, and as we do, Erevair squeezes my hand. "I'm glad you smell nice, Elly. It's much better than when you were stinky."

I'm not sure if he's chiding me, but either way it's kind of funny. Truth is, when my anxiety gets the better of me, it's easy to fall back into my old habits. No speaking, no socializing, and forming a fine crust of dirt over my skin so no one will notice me. But then I think of Bek, and how I don't want to be filthy when he comes home. I want him to be excited to see me. I want him to kiss me all over and touch me. I'm far more touchable clean.

Kae skips back with her basket in her hand. "Mama said extra eggs please."

I look up at the two women, and Kira waves at me with a smile, acknowledging us. She doesn't get up, though, and I don't head over. I get along better with the children, and everyone gives me enough space that I don't feel cornered. "More eggs?" I ask.

Kae nods as if that answers everything.

"It's for No-Poison Day," Erevair announces, twining his tail with Kae's again as she slips her little hand in his once more. "We're going to decorate eggs and make wishes."

Oh. I remember someone saying something about a bastardized

Christmas holiday, but I haven't paid much attention. Holidays are a very distant memory. I spent so long in cages and zoos that a lot of my Earth dreams are just very, very distant memories. It didn't occur to me to celebrate, not with Bek gone. "I see."

We head down the path in the canyon toward the dirtbeak cliffs, and as we do, Erevair chatters on and on about the holiday. "No-Poison Day is going to be the day after tomorrow. That's what Mama says. Is that a long time, Elly?"

I shake my head, content to let him ramble.

"Mama says if I am good that I can have a special present the night before and then another on the morning of. She said it won't be plants, though, because the No-Poison plants are saved for girls so their mates can kiss them. My papa's not here for Mama to kiss though, so I hope she doesn't have to kiss me." His face screws up.

"She won't," I tell him with a squeeze of his hand.

"We have garlands and pretty things hanging in our hut, though. And Mama said that Miss Stacy is going to cook special treats for everyone for the holiday. And we're going to play games like football, but we have to be careful not to play too hard, because Drenol is really old and Mama is afraid we'll hurt him." When I don't add more to this than a hand-squeeze to let him know that I'm listening, he turns to Kae. "I asked Mama if I could have a tunic just like Papa's favorite. Or a fishing net, but she says I'm too little for a fishing net and I'll just pull myself right under. What did you ask for, Kae?"

"For Papa to come home," Kae chirps. "That's the only thing I want."

I feel a dull ache in my heart. Oh, I want that, too. I want the hunters to come home and I want to see my strong, proud Bek stalk into the village, his gaze roaming over faces as he looks for me.

That's what I want, too—for my love, my mate, my everything, to return home to my arms.

Erevair makes an unhappy noise. "I don't think you'll get that, Kae. Mama says the brutal season will be here any day now and that means Papa and the others might not be back until the worst of the snows are over. That could be turns and turns and tuuu-urns of the moons. We might not see them until it's time for the bitter season again." He says all this with matter-of-fact authority, but each word is like a dagger in my heart.

It's already been weeks and weeks. The thought of being without Bek for months on end feels like torture. I want to cry. I want to turn around and crawl back into my bed and sleep until he gets back here. I'm so sad and lonely without him. It's breaking me.

"Elly?" Erevair shakes my hand again, making sure that I'm listening. He repeats his question. "What do you think of that?"

I think it's awful, but all I do is shrug. I can't speak. There's a huge knot in my throat.

"You should ask for something else, Kae," Erevair tells her. "Just in case it doesn't happen."

She thinks for a moment. "A new basket."

"That's a good answer," he says cheerily.

I wish I could be so easily distracted. I feel as if all of the air has been sucked out of the canyon. Bek not back for months. I thought…I thought with him as my mate, I'd never be alone again. Now it seems I'm alone just as much as I ever was, and it hurts more than I ever thought it would.

By the time we've filled our baskets, Erevair has told me and Kae in great detail about No-Poison Day and what he wants to get and what Bek gave him last year and how bad the snows are supposed to be very soon and it's like my spirit has been completely and utterly squashed by his childish chatter. I'm more than ready to go back to my hut and have myself a nice, long cry.

Kae walks carefully with the basket of eggs clutched to her chest, as if she's carrying valuable treasure, and so we head back slowly, so as not to jog her finds. Erevair doesn't mind this because it allows him to talk even more about his favorite subject—the upcoming holiday. It's like the quieter Kae is, the more Erevair has to fill the quiet space, and by the time we get back to the village, I'm relieved to see Claire greet us, her baby Relvi on her hip. "All done, sweetie?" She smiles at me. "I need you to come back and help Mama with her fire," Claire tells him, putting her hand out. "Get your share of the dirtbeak nests and we'll go wash your hands."

I set down my basket so he can fill his little backpack, which he does with great abandon. Claire wrinkles her nose at his enthusiasm, and chuckles when he prances ahead. "He's so excited about the holiday. I hope he didn't talk too much."

"Not too much," I lie.

"I told him if he was good and helpful, he'd get a special present." She grimaces. "Of course, now I have to think of something, but I'm sure it'll come to me. Are you okay? Erevair said you miss Bek a lot and I know it's hard when the guys are gone for a long time." Her kind gaze searches my face even as her baby grabs a fistful of her hair and raises it to her drooling mouth. "I'd say it gets easier over time, but I'm not sure it does. I think we just get more used to the silence and an empty hut. And of course, there are the kits.

When they come, it certainly isn't lonely. Tiring, yes. Quiet and lonely, no." She pulls her hair from Relvi's little fist and glances back where Erevair is skipping toward her hut. "Anyhow, I'm chattering on. I just wanted to say that I understand, and if you'd like to come to dinner, you're more than welcome. I love the company as much as Erevair does. He considers you family since you're Bek's, and of course I do too."

I'm not surprised at the generous offer. Claire's very sweet. This isn't the first time she's tried to get me to come over for dinner. I'm sure she senses my loneliness although I think some of it is just her generous heart. But I'm not entirely sure I'm ready to be social. It's hard enough just to answer people when they ask me a question. I'm sure I'll get there.

Just...not yet. And not without Bek.

So I shrug and give Claire a half smile, promising nothing. Kae takes that as a sign that the conversation is over and grabs my hand, dragging me forward to her mother's hut. I let myself be tugged along, even though I'm not entirely comfortable with being touched. I love it when it's Bek, and I tolerate it when it's the kids, because they don't know any better, and they'd just get hurt feelings if I freaked out. Besides, the kids always have sticky, sweaty, innocent hands. They're warm and soft and nothing like the hands that grabbed me when I was a slave. Even so, I have to force myself to focus on other things, because if I think about being touched for too long, it's going to send my brain to weird places. I focus on the sprawl of the village instead.

The morning's in full swing and that means everyone's out and about. I see Hemalo spreading his skins out in front of his tanning hut near the edge of the village. His mate Asha talks with him as he works, her toddler latched on to her breast and nursing. In the middle of the village, a few of the elders skin frozen carcasses, likely working on the trail rations that are a staple food around here. In the distance, I can see Ariana and Gail over at the longhouse, talking with a few of the children clustered around them. I'm guessing more of the women are going to be gathering by the central fire, as they usually do to talk, share mending, and eat Stacy's food.

I don't join them often. Gail tries to drag me to chat with the others, but it's too many people at once, and no comforting Bek to hide behind and cling to. I prefer to hide in my hut.

Kae gives my hand another little squeeze, directing me toward her mother's hut, and I'm unsurprised to see Kira's still out there, waiting for us. She's sitting on a little stool outside her front door instead of near the fire, her leatherwork still in her lap. She looks up at the sight of us, and her smile grows wide at the sight of little Kae with her basket. "Find a lot, did you, baby?"

Kae nods shyly and releases my hand, bringing her basket to her mother.

"Ooo, you did wonderful, honey." The normally solemn Kira gushes over the eggs as if she's never seen one before. "Look at what a great job you did." She kisses her daughter's silky brown hair. "Leave this with me and go catch up with the others. Miss Ariana's talking about math today. Isn't that exciting?"

"Yes!" Kae cries happily and hands the basket over, then races off towards the others at the far end of the village.

Kira watches her go, a smile on her face, and when Kae's out of earshot, she turns to me. "Someday she's going to learn that math isn't all that exciting. Until then, I love that she's so eager to learn." She gives me a faint smile. "Thank you for taking them today."

I nod and hold tight to the straps of my pack, wondering if it's rude to turn and just walk away. Probably. I stay, feeling awkward, because I'm not sure what else to do.

Kira pulls at her thick bone needle, dragging it through the hard leather. "Sometimes I think she's just like me, but then she'll say or do something that's pure Aehako, and it makes my heart so glad to see it. I'd rather her be like him than me. He's so full of joy and laughter." She sighs and a melancholy look crosses her face.

I recognize that look. That's the look of a woman that misses her mate. All at once, I feel like I've connected to Kira. I pull up the empty stool next to hers and sit down, dropping my loaded backpack behind me. It's like the dam's opening, because I can't not talk about how much I miss Bek. "He's been gone a while. Bek, I mean. Aehako, too."

Her nod is one of sympathetic understanding. "Not going to lie, I'm worried. I keep telling myself everything is fine, but then I wonder about the twenty in the pods and if they opened them after all or changed their minds. I wonder if those newcomers are coming here, or if they're all dead, or a million other scenarios that run through my mind." She sighs heavily. "I tell myself it's all fine and he'll be home soon enough, but sometimes the negative thoughts crawl in my head and don't go away." Kira stabs at the leather in her hands and gives her head a little shake. "Normally when I get all 'Debbie Downer,' Aehako's right there to pull me back out of it again, but he's not here. You know how it goes. They have to go out to hunt regularly, so I tell myself this is just like one of those times. Some days it helps."

"How do you stand it?" I whisper, hugging my arms against my furs. "I wish Bek never had to leave."

"Oh, I wish for things like that, too," Kira tells me in a soft voice. She tugs her thick needle and the leather "thread" through her project. "But I tell myself that I'm a realist. Our tribe is a hunter-gatherer one. He has to go hunt, not just to feed us, but to feed everyone. And he enjoys it. I also think that him leaving for a time and coming back allows us to miss each other. It gives him time to hunt and work with the hunters, and I get to spend some quality time with the other girls and the kits. It works out well, and it's good to have a bit of space." She pushes her needle into the tough leather again. "I just wish it would be less space right about now. I want him home."

I know the feeling. I think of Bek's face, his big body, and the way he holds me close, and I feel so lonely for him I could scream and cry all at once. "I don't have anyone but him," I say, and then feel like an idiot for confessing that. I have Gail. I have the other women in the village. Everyone's so nice to me...but it's not the same as Bek. Nothing is.

Kira gives me a sympathetic smile. "I know. It was really hard for me when I was newly pregnant with Kae. Aehako and I were mated, but things were still new. Every day that he was gone felt like the longest day of my life. I hate to sound all 'Mommy' on you, but it gets easier and harder once your kit arrives. You have a new, wonderful little person to occupy your time...and you hate that your mate has to leave all the more. But it's a good distraction at least." She glances down toward the longhouse. "Kae's been asking about her daddy a lot lately, and I don't have any answers. I'm glad the big holiday is coming up so she can focus on that and not on how long he's been gone. Right now I'm trying to focus on making No-Poison Day as good as I can possibly make it. There's going to be food and presents and games and Christmas carols and a story about a fat alien named Santa and his sleigh pulled by eight shiny dvisti." Her smile is wry. "We're going to get a tree tomorrow. Drenol and Kashrem are going with a few of the girls and their kits to help with the cutting. You're more than welcome to come along and pick out one of your own."

Maybe I will. It's been ten years since I had a Christmas tree or celebrated any sort of holiday. The idea's oddly appealing even if it hurts to think that I'm going to spend it without Bek. Maybe I'll just prepare our hut for the holiday like he's going to be there anyhow and not take any of the decorations down until he gets home. I kind of like that idea.

I clasp my hands tightly in my lap and glance at the leather as she gives it another vicious stab. "Is that a present for Kae?"

"Aehako, actually." She holds the leather up and I can see a big piece cut in the shape of a peanut. "New boots. He's rough on his and I'm making these with red laces because I think they look nice against the paler leather. I'm going to do a second layer inside with fur lining to keep his feet warm." Kira smooths her hand down the piece. "All the stabbing helps me take out my frustration, and when he gets home, he'll have a nice present. Win-win."

I like that idea. Even though I feel a little exposed and open right now for chatting so much with Kira, I love the thought of making Bek a gift with my hands. "Can...can you show me how?"

Kira looks surprised at my request. Of course she is. I'm the one that would rather hide in my hut than hang out with the village women. But there's something soothing about Kira's quiet, practical personality—and the fact that she feels the same way I do about our missing mates. Sitting with her's not so bad. I tried to be friendly with Maylak, since she's Bek's sister, but she watches me far too closely, and her mate is always nearby, and they have kits, and it's just too many people all at once. But here with Kira, it's not so bad.

"I can show you," Kira says after a momentary pause. "I have some extra leather. Do you have one of his old boots so we know what to cut to?"

Chagrined, I realize I don't, and shake my head.

She gives me a half smile. "It's all right. We can make yours large and add a place to lace it up. I've learned that it's a lot easier to cut down a piece of clothing that's too big than to add to one that's too small. We'll make them big and start from there. Come on."

# 3

**RAAHOSH**

I can handle a great deal of pain, or bitter cold, or a long journey away from home...but I cannot handle my fierce mate's pain at being told that others will be returning home and we will not. She bellowed her frustration to me at not being allowed to return home to our kits just yet. Then, her rage turned to bitter tears and she clung to me as she wept. It is the pregnancy hawr-moans, she tells me. They make her emotional.

I think it is more than that, though. She is sad and misses Aayla and Raashel. I miss them just as deeply as she does. I am just as frustrated as she is that we cannot return to the village. But I understand my chief's decision, even if I do not like it. I let him know my displeasure, and now there is nothing to do except hunt until my irritation eases. But my hunting partner, my Liz, is not interested in going out this day. She is too angry and wishes to stay in our tent and sulk. It is unlike her, but I know she misses our kits fiercely. And I think of her tears and how she clung to me, and...I wish to fix this.

I do not know how, but I will fix this. If I cannot bring her home to her young, I must do something that will bring her back to the teasing, clever mate that I love so well. It makes me ache to see her so defeated.

I head out to the beach, and as I do, I hear the quiet sound of sobbing. Har-loh, who is just as upset that she cannot see her kit as my Liz is. A moment later, Rukh emerges from their small cave, frustration plain on his face. He rakes his shaggy hair back from his face and then storms toward me, furious. "This is not right," he declares. "We go home."

"We cannot go," I tell him flatly. "Much as I would like to leave, we are needed here. You know this. Liz and your Har-loh know this, too. They are just heavy with kit and sad. They will not risk the lives of these newcomers, no matter how much they might miss their kits." There is a knot in my throat, because I miss my kits, too. Bah. I think of little Aayla and her round, happy little face and shining eyes. I think of my Raashel, who is far too clever, like her mother. She would greet me with her little sly smile and then search my pockets, looking for the small treats and presents I would bring her.

And I ache deep inside, because I want to hold them close and tell them of how much I have missed them, but I must wait longer still. I know they are safe. I cannot be too upset. Well, I can be a little upset. I would rather be with them than feeding these useless ones. But it must be done, and the newcomers wish to learn. We must be patient for a little longer.

Rukh growls. "I miss my son."

"I miss my daughters," I tell my brother. "But I cannot worry over them right now. I know they are safe and looked after in the village. It is my Liz that is my concern right now."

Rukh crosses his arms and grunts, his jaw set in frustration. "My Har-loh will not stop crying."

I know the helpless feeling. My mate wanted to make this No-Poison Day special for our daughters because we have another kit on the way very soon. Now we will not even be home to celebrate it. I think of the little gifts that Liz has been making around the fire each night. We can send them with the others on their journey, but it will not be the same as watching their faces when they get their gifts. My heart hurts at the thought, but I know Liz must be aching even more. She enjoys being at my side, but at the same time, she feels torn that she cannot be with the girls.

I hate that she feels regret. That she feels trapped here, away from our kits.

We must do something to bring smiles back to our mates' faces.

"Let us bring No-Poison here," Rukh says suddenly.

I clasp a hand on his arm, because he has said exactly what I was thinking. "A fine idea, my brother. We can look for plants close to camp and make bundles of them for our mates."

"What else?" Rukh asks.

I do not remember. Most of it is foolishness, but my mate enjoys it. I rub my chin, thinking. "Perhaps we should ask some of the humans for suggestions."

Rukh nods at the distant shore. I turn and look, and two humans stand on the sandy beach. One is Tee-ah, the young female. She talks to the one with the four-armed mate. I rack my mind, trying to recall her name. They all look the same to me—Not-Liz. It takes me a moment to remember—Lo-ren. I gesture for Rukh to follow and jog my way down toward the edge of the water.

The two humans stand and chatter, unaware of our approach. Lo-ren holds the motherless kit on her hip, talking to Tee-ah as she does. They watch the water, and a quick glance out shows that Lo-ren's four-armed mate, K'thar, is learning to cast nets into the surf with Zolaya. It is a wise task for him to take on, because the strange male is extremely strong. After another cast of the nets deep into the water, he turns to his mate and makes a shivering motion, and then rolls his neck. This cool weather is new to his people. The humans said that the entire island was warm and steamy like the fruit cave. It sounds terrible.

"Ho," I call out, doing my best to sound friendly.

The females turn to look at me, wariness on their faces as Rukh and I approach. I do not blame them. Normally I only speak to the humans to correct them on something they are doing wrong. Perhaps I am not the most patient of hunters. I hear Zolaya calling K'thar's attention back to the nets—no doubt the protective male is ready to come and get between me and his mate if I make her upset. "I have a question. It is about human things," I say, and do my best to be…well, if not pleasant, less fearsome.

"Human things?" Lo-ren echoes, bouncing the kit on her hip as she glances out to the waters and to her mate. "What sorts of human things?"

"We wish to know about No-Poison," Rukh says.

"What?" Tee-ah blurts out, a confused expression on her face.

"The holiday," I explain. "The one with the leaves and the kissing and the gifts."

The two females exchange a glance. "Um, humans have a lot of holidays," Lo-ren says.

I bite back my impatience. This is for Liz. "It is the holiday with the gifts," I repeat, talking slowly. "With the tree and the strings of decorations."

"And kissing," Rukh adds.

Tee-ah giggles. Lo-ren gives her a quelling look and steps in front of her, a hint of a smile touching her mouth. "I'm going to assume you guys mean Christmas. Like Christmas trees and Santa Claus and giving presents, right?"

"What does that have to do with poison and kissing?" Tee-ah whispers loud enough for me to hear, but Lo-ren swats her with a hand and focuses her gaze on me, waiting.

At least one of these females is sensible. I ignore the silly, giggly one. "Yes. My mate is sad she cannot be home with our kits for the holiday and so I wish to give her the holiday here."

"Aww, that's sweet," Tia says with another giggle. "I love it."

"I—we," I correct, pointing at Rukh, "wish to know how we can bring the holiday to our mates and make them smile."

"Foot-ball games?" Rukh asks, gravely serious. "Eggs?"

Lo-ren looks even more puzzled. "Uh, okay. No, I wouldn't start with those things. I'd start with gifts for your mates."

"We will have something for them," I say and give her an impatient flick of my hand. "Tell me of your traditions. Your customs. I need more of those."

"Oh, um, all right. I'm guessing a big red suit and white beard is out. You could do a tree, though, and decorate it. Make it look festive." Lo-ren adjusts the wraps around the kit on her hip as she speaks.

"With a star on top," Tee-ah adds. "Gotta have a star."

I do not know what she means by that, but I will figure it out. I look over at Rukh and he nods. We can do a tree. "What else?" I ask.

"Let's see...presents, gifts," Lo-ren says, pondering. "A family meal. Christmas carols!"

"Oooh, yes," Tee-ah adds and claps her hands. "That would be perfect."

"How is your singing voice?" Lo-ren asks.

It is not good. "Cay-rols are important to the holiday?"

"Very," Tee-ah insists.

Then they must be done. "Teach me these songs." I will learn them all and sing them to my mate to show her I care.

# 4

**ELLY**

I decide I'm going to give Christmas to Bek. Maybe he won't be here for No-Poison Day to celebrate officially with the tribe, but that doesn't matter. Kira helps me with the boots and I spend all night sewing because I'm too distracted to sleep for a change. When dawn comes, I head out and join the others on their tree-hunting expedition. They're not close to the trees we had at home, but I take a little pink one anyhow, make a stand for it, and then spend hours sitting in front of Kira's hut with her and Kae and Erevair, making garlands from dried seeds. By the time the suns set that day, my hut is decorated, and I curl up on the blankets once more to work on Bek's boots. After the boots, I want to make him a tunic. Maybe some special trail ration cakes he can take with him the next time he goes out. I can think of a million things my mate needs now that I sit down and really focus on him, and I want to make him everything.

When he gets home, I'll be ready to celebrate with him, and the thought brings me joy and renewed purpose. If he can't be here with me, I can still bask in his love.

# 5

**BEK**

"I need a new loincloth after that bit of travel," Aehako tells me with a nervous laugh as we slide to the ground from the dragon's back. He kneels in the snow and presses his horned brow to the ground. "I never thought I would be so glad to see snow underfoot."

"Didn't like air travel?" Vuh-ron-ca asks sweetly, her hand patting the golden dragon's scales. "My poor Ashtar. So misunderstood."

The dragon snorts and lowers one massive shoulder to let her down off his back. Over on the far side of the creature, Vektal and Rokan steady themselves, looking as ill at ease as I feel. My stomach is still gurgling unpleasantly from the ride over.

Hard to believe that the male called Ash-tar can turn into such a thing. Bigger than two sky-claw together, he is a massive predator of claws and scales and fanged teeth—and wings. It is like nothing

I have ever seen before, but Vuh-ron-ca assures us that this is normal for his people. Ash-tar has told her all about it, and judging from how at ease she is with his strange, gargantuan form, this is not the first time she has encountered him as a dragon.

When I first heard that Ash-tar would be our travel, I thought I misunderstood. Then I worried that Vektal's mind had perhaps gone soft, because the golden male is tall, but he is no stronger than any sa-khui male. I did not imagine how he would carry us and so quickly. Of course, I could never imagine that he would shift into such a creature. He is like nothing on this world...which should not surprise me, and yet does. For all his size and fierce demeanor, though, Ash-tar is extremely careful with his human mate, making sure she was seated well and covered up before he took off into the air.

And so we were carried on a dragon's back through the air, in a leather pack of sorts that had two pouches hanging off each side of the dragon. Each hunter rode inside a pouch, surrounded with bags of supplies. Vuh-ron-ca calls it a "modified saddle" and explained that her people—humans—used to ride atop of animals much like Farli's Chahm-pee, but such a suggestion seems ridiculous to me. The dvisti is dumb and skittish and smells bad. I do not understand why anyone would ride atop it when feet are perfectly fine. But...it is also hard to believe that we have made many days of travel and crossed over the mountains in one afternoon. Ash-tar could fly so high in his creature form that no obstacles stood in our way. The wind was biting to the bone at so high up, no matter how many layers I put over my body, but I cannot say that I am displeased.

If I must ride a monster to get to my Ell-ee, I will do so gladly.

The suns are setting in the distance, and here we are, at the lip of the gorge. It is oddly quiet, but cookfires thread plumes of smoke up from the gorge itself, so I know there are people below. Why does no one come to greet us?

"I think they're scared of the dragon," Vuh-ron-ca states, kneeling near a pack and opening it up, then shaking out a long, heavy fur cloak. She gets to her feet and holds it out. "Come on and change, babe. You're scaring the locals."

The enormous dragon makes a chuffing sound that might be laughter and tucks his massive wings in close against his body. Then, in the blink of an eye, the dragon is gone and Ash-tar is kneeling in the snow, naked and sweaty. The leather packs strapped across his back fall to the ground and Vuh-ron-ca moves to his side, wrapping him in the cloak and pressing a kiss to his face as he pulls her against him. "You did great, babe," she tells him.

"I know," he says, an arrogant smile playing on his mouth as he glances over at us. He is amused at how terrified we were at his flight.

I do not care. All I care about is that we are home and somewhere below, my Ell-ee waits for me. "Come," I say, impatient. "Let us pick up our packs and go. I did not fly on the back of a monster all day to sit here at the entrance to the valley all night."

"Grab a pack," Vektal says. "For once, Bek is right."

"My thanks for the confidence," I retort. I do not mind his words, though. I am going home to my mate, and that is all that matters.

We each take some of the packs that were sent along with us. For those that were not allowed to return home on this trip, gifts and small treats were sent along from the Icehome camp. There are packs of shells for kits, salt for cooking, and a few frozen crawlers for meals, as well as bundles of fur and gifts of dried foods. It is a small comfort for those left behind, and I think of Liz's and

Raahosh's sad faces when they found out there was no room for them to come. I will make sure to give their gifts to their kits and tell them how much their parents miss them.

"Ready?" Vektal asks, glancing around at our small group. I am curious as to why he would ask such a thing, and then I realize that Ash-tar is hovering very protectively over Vuh-ron-ca, who looks nervous. I wonder if she is like my Ell-ee in that she is anxious around new people. Wise of Vektal to try and ease their worries.

"Let us go see who is brave enough to greet us, eh?" Aehako sings out, all cheerfulness once more. "I would wager my best fur tunic that it will be Sessah, ready to shake his spear at us."

I snort at that, because in my mind, Sessah is still a kit clinging to his mother's tunic.

"All will be well," Rokan promises. He has been quiet on this journey, and I wonder at his thoughts.

We take our packs and lower them down the pulley, then head down in groups. I go down with Aehako and Rokan, and Vektal stays close to Vuh-ron-ca and Ash-tar. I do wonder who will be coming to greet us. The elders? Kashrem and Hemalo? Sessah? There are not many hunters left in the village as of late, and the ones that are will be determined to protect their mates. I do not blame them. I should never have left my Ell-ee's side. I have regretted it every day since. If Warrek and Harrec could stay behind because they were newly resonated, it should not matter that I had only a turn of the moon more with my mate. She is far more fragile in spirit than their mates. But then I feel guilty for thinking such a thing, because is my Ell-ee not strong and brave? It is only my longing that makes me worry over her. She is a survivor. She will be fine without me...and perhaps that is what worries me the most. That she will have decided she no longer needs me at her side. That she will be a different person when I return and even resonance will not anchor her to my side.

I rub my chest, wishing for the friendly hum of my khui that would tell me she is near, and that I am wanted.

A band of hunters appears at the far end of the canyon, spears in hand. I can make out Oshen's age-rolled shoulders, and the two next to him must be Vadren and Drayan, with Drenol and Vaza behind them. I snort with amusement at that. Have the elders decided to come and protect the village and left the able-bodied hunters behind to protect their mates? It is admirable...and a little foolish as well.

Aehako raises a hand in the air, jogging forward. "Ho, Father. It is us! No need to be afraid."

"My sons?" Oshen calls out, squinting as he steps forward.

"It is us, Father," Rokan agrees, moving to Aehako's side. "We have journeyed back."

"But where are the rest?" Vadren asks, studying our small group. His braids are stark white against his skin and the hand that holds his spear trembles just a little, but he keeps himself strong and upright, a fierce look on his weathered face as he studies Vuh-ron-ca and Ash-tar. "What of the giant creature in the sky? And who are these newcomers?"

"There is much to explain," Vektal says briskly, moving forward. "But everyone is well and sends their greetings. It is good to see all of you."

The elders cluster around us, offering to take packs and greeting the Icehome newcomers with pleasantries. I watch Aehako and Rokan hug their father and wonder if my sister and her family are well...but I mostly think of my Ell-ee. She is the one I truly want to see. "If we are done shaking our spears at each other, let us go home," I announce, but everyone is busy exclaiming over Ash-tar's scale-like golden skin and the packs of goods we carry. They are in no hurry, it seems.

Annoyed, I shoulder my pack and head on toward the village. They do not need me here for greetings. They are just fine without me. I head on through the canyon, my steps quickening as I round the bend and catch sight of the village at the far end of the gorge. The smoke from the fires has disappeared, and all of the huts have privacy screens in front of them. In the distance, I see a few hunters standing in front of the longhouse, armed with spears. No doubt they are still frightened at the appearance of the dragon.

Bah. The time for protectiveness is past. I cup a hand to my mouth, calling out for my mate. "Ell-ee! It is I, your Bek! I am home!"

"Bek?" A startled shriek rises from behind the wall of hunters standing in the doorway of the longhouse, and then a small figure wiggles out from underneath Haeden's shoulder and races toward me. It is my mate, covered in furs, her pale face all eyes and pointed chin, and she is the most beautiful thing I have ever seen. My khui races at the sight of her, and my knees grow weak. I feel the overwhelming urge to weep like a female, I am so relieved to see her alive and well.

She sobs as she runs toward me, her arms outstretched, and I drop my packs on the ground. I do not care if the delicate shells inside are crushed—all that matters is getting my arms around my sweet mate and holding her close.

Ell-ee slams into me with all of the weight of her slight form, and her arms go around my neck. "Bek!" she cries, and buries her face against my neck. She sobs my name over and over, her body shaking even as she wraps her thin legs around my waist, as if she is terrified I will leave again.

My mate.

The hollow parts inside me suddenly feel full once more. The bitterness I carried for these long days without her is gone, and I touch her hair, her back, her leg, petting her and reassuring myself that it is her after all. "My Ell-ee," I murmur, and my voice is husky with emotion. "How I have missed you."

"Never leave me again," she weeps against my throat, her hands tangling in my hair. "You're not allowed."

"Never," I agree. Even if I must go on the trails hunting, I will take her with me. The thought of leaving her again is unbearable.

She lifts her face and her cheeks are streaked with half-frozen tears, but she is smiling. She is so lovely that it steals the breath from my throat. Our khuis sing loud at our reunion, and I feel a surge of lust at the sight of her.

*Mine. My mate.*

I press my mouth to hers. It has been far too long since I've tasted her. To my delight, my normally shy Ell-ee responds with a hungry little moan, clutching my face as she kisses me with ferocious intent. There is nothing better than a mate eager for my touch, and I return her kiss with equal intensity, our mouths hungry as they lock together. There is nothing that exists beyond Ell-ee's slight form pressed against me, her tongue slicking against mine.

I have waited too long to claim her again, and I will wait no longer. I ignore the happy cries of those around us reuniting with family. Nearby, I hear Aehako laugh as he swings his daughter into his arms, and Vektal calls out for Shorshie. Others crowd around, wanting to know about family members and greet the newcomers, but I care for none of this. With my Ell-ee in my arms, I push through the crowd, heading for our hut.

I am going to claim my mate and fill her body with my seed. Greeting the rest of the tribe can wait.

She makes hungry little noises as I carry her away, her legs tight around my hips. I have missed this—missed *her*—so much that it makes my spirit ache. It is like I have become whole once more and must take my fill of her to wipe away the memories of those endless nights and days without her at my side.

We make it to our hut, and I kick aside the privacy screen. The fire inside is nothing but banked coals, and our furs remain in the same spot as they always are. I move to the bed of furs and gently lay my mate down amongst them.

Ell-ee whimpers when I let her go, clinging to me. "No," she whispers, urgent. "Stay."

I groan when she slicks her little tongue against the seam of my mouth. There is nothing I want more than to stay. "I must put the privacy screen back up so we will be undisturbed." Even for a moment, the idea of leaving the warmth of her arms seems like a poor choice. But then I think of the others coming in and disturbing us when I am cock-deep into my mate, and I growl at the thought. I wish to see no one but her until dawn tomorrow, at the very least. I force myself to get up from the furs, ignoring the tempting brush of her fingers down my arm, and cross the hut with haste. I slap the screen over the entrance, shove a basket behind it so it cannot budge, and then return to my mate's waiting arms.

"I've missed you so much," Ell-ee breathes. Her eyes glimmer with unshed tears. "I feel like we've been apart more than we've been together."

"That changes this day," I vow to her. "I will not leave you alone again. This I swear." I take her hand and press my mouth to her palm. "Being without you made every day difficult."

She nods, her eyes so full of sadness. "It was hard to get out of bed sometimes, knowing that you wouldn't be there. I had to force myself to eat, too."

The thought brings me pain. I picture her, thin and miserable, and pull her close to me. "You must be strong for our kit, my Ell-ee. For me and for him."

"I know," she says in a soft voice, and her fingers flutter along my jaw. "But sometimes it's really hard."

All the more reason to never leave her again. Perhaps she is not as independent as Leezh, or as outgoing as Mah-dee, but it does not matter. She is strong in different ways, and she needs me to feel whole. I understand this—how many mornings did I wake up and feel as if I was hollow without her at my side? "From now on," I tell her, "when I go to hunt, you will come with me. If I must return to the Icehome shores, we will go together."

"You promise?" Her thumb skims over my mouth.

"I vow it." I nip the tip of her finger. "I need you as much as you need me."

"Good." She strokes a lock of hair back from my brow. "And when the kit comes…?"

"We will stay wherever we must until you can travel again. I mean it when I say I will never leave your side again." I undo the knotted band holding her first layer of furs wrapped around her torso. "We are together, always. The others will have to accept this."

"We can go back to the other tribe—the Ice home, you called them? —if you are needed." She bites her lip, uncertain.

"No one needs me as much as you, my mate," I tell her. "And the same holds true for me. I need you more than anything."

With a happy sigh, Ell-ee caresses my face as I pull at her layers of clothing. Like all the humans, she covers herself in heavy wraps of fur to keep warm, and finding her soft skin underneath is a challenge. She helps me with the clothing, sitting up and watching me with eager eyes as I pull her boots off and then remove her leggings. Next, her tunic goes, and then the band that covers her slight teats. When she is bare and laid out before me, I breathe out a sigh of pure joy. I am a fool for ever leaving her side.

Ell-ee reaches for me, tugging at the heavy wrap I wear over my shoulders. "You're all covered up," she whispers. "I want to touch you."

I strip off my layers, casting them aside until I am in nothing but my loincloth and my boots. She sits up in bed and tugs at the knot at my waist that keeps my loincloth in place, and her hands skim over my hard, aching cock. A groan escapes my throat. "Do not," I murmur, catching her hand in mine. "It has been too long since I have touched you. I must keep my control or else I will not make this very good for you."

For some reason, that makes Ell-ee give a throaty laugh. "Is that supposed to discourage me? I *like* the thought of making you crazy, Bek. I dream about it all day long."

"You do?" I am astonished. I think about new and exciting ways to touch her constantly, but I did not realize she did the same.

She nods and gives me an excited look, squirming on the blankets with enthusiasm. "I think about when I put my hands on you and you make that noise in your throat." She lays her palms against my chest, and I suck in a breath. “Like that,” she murmurs. “And I think about what noises you’d make if I put my mouth on you.”

Is she suggesting...I groan at the thought. “Ell-ee.”

“I want to do it,” she tells me. “Can I? Will you let me?”

Will I let her? I can think of nothing else but that, now that she has called my attention to it. “Only if you wish to.”

“Being with you makes me wish to do a great many things,” she says, and she pulls my loincloth free, exposing my cock to the air.

She looks at my cock with such hungry eyes that it makes my entire body twitch in response. Her small, soft hands curl around my length, her odd-colored skin so vibrant against my dark blue. I love the sight of her fingers against my skin...almost as much as I love her touch. "I always forget how big you are," she murmurs in that soft, shy voice of hers. "And when I see you, it always surprises me. In a good way, of course." She flicks her gaze up to me and gives me a bashful smile.

"I feel the same when I look at you, my Ell-ee," I tell her. "I forget how lovely you are, and then when I look at you, you take the air from my lungs."

Her cheeks go pink with pleasure and she licks her lips. "I love you," she whispers. "I'm so glad you're home."

I want to tell her of all the days I missed her, of how hard it was to be separated from her after I've found her, of what torture the long nights were, of how I worried over her, hating that she was here alone and that she might need me—but everything flies from my mind when she leans forward, her rounded bottom going into the air even as her mouth descends on my cock.

I...have never felt something as good as this. The hot, wet suction of her mouth as she closes over the head of my cock...it is an indescribable pleasure. I make a noise that is neither sigh nor gasp, but something garbled in between. Her soft mane falls over my lap, caressing my thighs even as she works her mouth over my length, exploring me with her lips.

Ell-ee's hand curls around my shaft, her other resting on my thigh. She kisses the head of my cock and then moves her mouth, trailing it up and down my skin, her tongue flicking at a thick vein on the underside. I try to remain still so I do not interrupt, but I cannot help but twitch in response every time her tongue touches against my skin. "Your skin is very soft here," she whispers to me. "And it smells like you." She sighs and rubs her face against my length, and I nearly spill my seed all over her face and mane at that small gesture.

A groan escapes me and I reach out to brush her mane back from her cheeks, because I want to look at her as she touches me. I want to see if she finds this as pleasurable as I do. No matter how good it feels, if she does not look pleased, we will stop and I will put my mouth between her legs, because I know she likes that. But her eyes are closed and there is an expression of soft joy on her face as she touches me. Her fingers skim up and down my length in fluttering caresses, and when a drop of my seed crowns on the head of my cock, she leans in and tastes it with her tongue.

And I must clench my fists so I do not lose control. My breath rasps in my throat, hard and rough. "Ell-ee," I growl. "Your mouth...it is too good. Let me pleasure you instead."

"No," she insists, her stubborn streak showing. "I want to do this for you. I like this. Aren't you enjoying it?" She looks up at me, worried. "Am I doing it wrong?"

"I do not think there is a wrong, my mate. If it feels good, that is all that matters." I reach out and caress her cheek. "And it feels very, very good."

She smiles up at me, pleased.

"Perhaps too good. I would give you pleasure instead." It is difficult to say the words, because she is already leaning over me once more, taking my cock into her mouth. Just that small motion is terribly distracting, and when her tongue glides along my shaft, I clench my fists and try to concentrate on less pleasing things so I do not spill my seed too soon and ruin her fun.

"You can," she says after a moment. "When I'm done with you. It doesn't have to be either-or." Ell-ee chuckles, her breath whispering over my skin. "We can do both."

I groan. She is too much, my sweet mate. I touch my hand to her mane, and when she makes an eager noise and takes me into her mouth again, I resist the urge to guide her head, to pump into the hot well of her mouth with my cock, to claim it like I do her cunt. The thought is a starkly appealing one, but my Ell-ee is fragile. I cannot—

But then her fingers glide up to my spur and I lose control. She teases it, rubbing the length gently with her fingers, and the breath explodes from my body. I growl again, my hand twisting in her silky mane, and I cannot resist rocking forward, thrusting into her mouth. She makes a little sound of eager pleasure, looking up at me with hot eyes. She likes it, and she wants more. I will give her more, then. I groan as she clasps one hand around my shaft and sucks me back into her mouth. She increases the sensation, using her tongue and licking me eagerly, making little pleasure noises as she does. I cannot help myself; I push into her mouth again, and when she encourages me to do so again, I thrust back into her mouth. It feels incredible, and the realization that she enjoys it as much as I do doubles the pleasure I feel. I pump into the soft, wet heat of her mouth again, and it feels like I am stroking into her cunt. My people do not do this, but I have heard humans have no such problem, and the realization that my Ell-ee wishes to take me every way possible is a heady one. I am gentle as I stroke into her eager mouth, but as she caresses my spur and touches my sac, my movements become shaky, my motions less gentle. She encourages me, and then I am thrusting into her mouth, on the verge of my release, even as she whimpers and makes delighted sounds, ready for my seed. I want to come inside her, but she is so frantic with her mouth, so ready, so willing, that I cannot pull myself away from the delicious sensation, even for a moment. I thrust in again, and again, and when she rubs her tongue along the underside of my cockhead once more, I lose all control.

I come inside her mouth, spilling on her tongue and lips. She gasps even as I groan, and when I try to pull free to finish my release, she grabs my tail and holds me in place, and I give her every last drop of my seed. It paints her mouth and chin, and she swallows, then licks her lips. "Oh, Bek," she whispers as she uses her tongue and fingers to lap up my spend. "I liked that so much."

"You did?" I am fascinated by this, by how giving my mate is. I came in her mouth. It seems...wrong, but I liked it far too much for it to be something bad. Nothing is bad between us. "It is not the sa-khui way."

"Maybe it should be." The tip of her tongue slicks along her upper lip. "I loved it. I loved watching you get so turned on, and when you put your hand in my hair..." She gives a little shiver of delight.

I groan again, because even though I have just finished, she makes me hard with need once more. My cock stirs just as my khui does, and this time, I wish to pleasure her. With a low growl, I grab her by the waist and bear her back to the furs, trailing my mouth down her belly. She is thinner than I remember, my Ell-ee, and I resolve I will never leave her side again. I will make sure she eats all the time, until she is as round and plump as Mah-dee. I like that thought very much. I press kisses to the soft, pale skin of her belly, moving lower until I brush my lips over the curls of her cunt. Her scent is sweetest here, and I know her curls hide the pink flush of her folds, the wet, rich flavor of her. My mouth waters for a taste, and when she moans and her hands go to my horns, her thighs trembling, I understand why she enjoyed giving me pleasure with her mouth. When I do the same for her, there is nothing better in the world.

And then I place my mouth on the soft flesh of her cunt, and she cries out, her body arching underneath me. A burst of wetness touches my tongue, telling me that she enjoys this as much as I enjoy her responses. There is a saying amongst the hunters—that there is no taste better than that of a resonance mate on your tongue, and I know this to be true. I have missed the taste of my sweet Ell-ee these long days apart. I have missed the taste of her, the scent of her need, the clench of her thighs as she presses against the sides of my face and horns. I glide one hand down her flank, caressing her. She has no tail for me to grasp onto, but I wind my tail around her ankle, clasping her against me. Her legs tremble and quiver as my tongue glides over her folds, and I can hear her breathing quickening with nervous anticipation. Ell-ee sucks in a breath when I explore her, teasing my mouth all along her cunt, but avoiding the best part—that sensitive third nipple at the top of her folds that she loves to be touched so much. I want to savor her first, to make her wild with need.

"Bek," she pants, her teats heaving. "Please. Come inside me. I want you to fill me up."

"Patience," I tell her, pleased that she is so needy. My khui rumbles with pleasure at the sight of her sprawled below me, her thighs clasping against my face. My mate. My perfect female, full of my kit and so wonderfully responsive to my touch. Resonance has chosen wisely for me, and I feel a burst of pride just looking at her. Ah, my sweet Ell-ee. So utterly perfect.

Mine. All mine.

With a grin of pure joy, I lower my head and go back to kissing and licking her cunt. I explore her with my mouth, though I have been between her thighs many times since we first mated. It does not matter. Every time is a delicious journey, and I love to feel her squirming underneath me, lifting her hips in silent guidance of where she wants my mouth most. I tease my tongue at the entrance to her core, where she is wettest, and when she moans my name, I give her a lick and then move away again, delighting in her whimper. I will pleasure her there, but in time. My cock already aches and grows hard with need once more, but I ignore it. It has been too long since I pleasured my Ell-ee, and I want to enjoy my time between her thighs.

I could spend all night here and never grow tired of her little sighs, her whimpers, her moans. I glance up at her even as I trace one finger up and down her wet seam, and her head is thrown back in the furs, her eyes closed. Her teats thrust into the air, nipples tight and pink, and as I watch, she rolls her hips, a silent request for more.

How can a male refuse such a pretty thing? I lower my head and press a kiss to the little nub of her third nipple, and she gives a little cry that makes my sac tighten in response. Ah, how I love that sound. I slide my finger back and forth along her folds, teasing her even as I tongue her nipple, making wet circles around it. She cries out, hips undulating underneath me, pressing up against my finger as I stroke nearer to her core. She wants to be pierced by it—by my body. She wants to be speared on my length, to have me fill her up.

By the snows, I want that, too. But I want the taste of her release on my tongue first, like she gave to me. I picture her mouth, shiny and painted with my seed, and groan deep. It renews my fever for her, and I apply myself with ferocity, tonguing her nipple with rapid, repeated strokes even as I pump a finger into her warmth.

"Oh! Bek! Oh, I want you so much," she cries out, and it is the loudest I have ever heard my mate. I groan at this, rocking my hips into the furs as if it were the clasp of her body. I am desperate to be inside her, but I need her to come first. I need it more than I have needed anything in this moment. I know my Ell-ee's body well, though, and I know for her to come, I must not falter. So I ignore her cries and her sweet begging, I ignore the rock of her hips and continue to lap at her third nipple with sure, steady strokes, even as I pump my finger inside her, mimicking the way my cock will fill her shortly. She arches and writhes up against my mouth, her hands gripping my horns. Her breath comes in short, sharp pants, but she is no longer begging for me. She has no air left for words. I can feel the quivers racing through her body, the way her thighs tense against my shoulders, and I know she is close. I add a second finger when I stroke into her heat, and continue with my tongue. Over and over, I flick it in a steady, unhurried rhythm against her most sensitive spot even as she goes wild underneath me.

Then, with a little scream of pleasure, my mate comes. Her body shudders against my face, and I taste a rush of wet warmth against my tongue. Her cunt clamps down against my fingers and I keep stroking her, determined to wring out every bit of pleasure possible. She moans and rubs up against me, rocking even as she shudders, until she is spent and panting, her pale skin glazed with a light sheen of sweat.

My Ell-ee is the most beautiful thing I have ever seen like this, sprawled and content underneath me. I press a kiss to the inside of her thigh, well pleased at her response. "I have missed that, my mate."

She gives a long, trembling sigh. "Oh, Bek."

I love the contented sound of her sigh. "I am here, my Ell-ee."

"Good." She curls her toes and stretches her arms over her head, then slides them back down to caress my face. "I missed you far too much. Missed this. Missed everything."

I kiss her thigh again, then continue upward, pressing a brief kiss at her curls before moving to her belly, and then up to her teats. They are small but perfect. I toy with the sensitive nipples and drag my tongue over them as she murmurs my name. Did I miss her? Like breathing. Have I dreamed of this? Every night. But I am here now, and my cock is a brief span away from where it belongs. I move over her, letting my larger weight settle carefully against her body. I prop myself up with my elbows so I do not crush her, and when she slides her legs apart wide in welcome, it feels as if I am truly home.

I rub the head of my cock against her slick folds, and then sink deep. Her sigh of pleasure is almost as wonderful as the hot clasp of her cunt around my length. I groan and hold her tightly against me, kissing her face as I ease into her. My Ell-ee is always tight, and no matter how deep I push with my initial thrust, I must always work my way deeper with slow, careful motions so she can take all of me. I push shallowly into her, rocking my hips as I whisper her name, and she digs her nails into my shoulders, closing her eyes and giving herself over to me with such trust that it makes my spirit ache with how much I love her.

And then I am seated fully inside her, and it feels...perfect. She sucks in a shuddering breath and then squirms underneath me. "Your spur," she murmurs, shifting. I know that it rubs against her third nipple, and the very sensation makes her crazed with need.

She is already sensitive there, and this will just add more to it. I know that my Ell-ee can come at least twice before I do, and I am determined to make sure that when I pump her full of my seed once more, she is right there with me, clenched tight in her own release. When she comes hard, she bites at my skin.

I love that. I want it again.

So I do everything I can to ensure that our joining is all about her pleasure. I take one of her hands and stretch it over her head, making her arch underneath me. She opens her eyes and watches me, her lips parted. With every thrust, she gives a little gasp, as if I am giving her brand new sensations every time and she does not know what to make of them. Her eyes locked to mine is intense, and every time I slide deep into the clasp of her body, it feels a little more intense with our gazes locked. As I thrust into her, I take my time, moving slow at first, and then speeding up. I flick my tail along her leg, teasing her because I know she is ticklish and more touches just add to her pleasure.

My Ell-ee does not keep her hand over her head for long. She pushes back against my grip and then whimpers when I thrust deep. Her hands come up and she clasps them against the sides of my face, as if she needs to anchor herself to me. "My Bek," she whispers, and there is such love and intense devotion in her eyes that it breaks my control. I want to go slow, but I cannot. Not when she looks at me as if I have placed the stars in the skies for her enjoyment alone. Fast and hard, I claim my mate, pumping into her slick heat with one forceful thrust after another, until we are moving across the furs with the clash of our bodies. She clings to me, utterly silent except for small sounds of pleasure that let me know she is here with me, riding this. Wild with my desire for her, I claim Ell-ee over and over with every stroke, as if I could paint into my soul the way she looks at me in this moment.

Her body clenches tight under my assault, and she arches under me, her mouth parting wide, her blue eyes seeming to grow darker with the force of her need. I hear her khui's thrumming song grow louder, and then my mate clutches at my neck, burying her face against my chest as she comes, her cunt tight and rippling around my length. With a shout of pleasure, I give in to my own release, emptying all of my desire for her into her welcoming body. When I have come so hard that it feels as if all of the seed has been wrung from my cock, I collapse on top of her, holding her close as our sweaty skin sticks together. She wraps her arms even tighter around me, pressing her mouth to my neck as she shivers with the aftershocks of her release.

It takes several long moments before she stops her trembling, and I roll over onto my side and tuck her body against me protectively. I cannot stop kissing her, though. Her eyes are closed and she looks tired and sated, but I kiss her brow and her nose over and over, fascinated by her delicate features and feeling as if I am the luckiest male alive because such a perfect female is mine. It is incredible to think how much my life has changed since she came into it.

To think that I once wanted a mate—any mate. Now I feel foolish that I would have settled for anyone less than her. Of course my khui waited many long turns of the seasons for her. It is far wiser than I am.

# 6

**AEHAKO**

My Kira looks well. I am relieved to see her standing tall and proud, and I grab her and swing her around in my arms at the sight of her. She laughs and bats at me playfully, encouraging me to put her down. I do not, and pull her close to me instead, holding her tight, my hand cupping her head. I have not slept at all since Rokan insisted that I return with Bek and Vektal. My mind has gone through all kinds of terrible scenarios, wondering what could possibly be wrong. Is my Kira unwell? Has something happened to my solemn little Kae? Or is it the village itself? Is that why I am needed at home? But now that I have my mate—whole and smiling—in my arms, the knot of worry that seems to have lodged permanently between my shoulders eases a little.

And yet...Rokan is never wrong.

I set my mate down on the ground and then give her a fierce kiss. Her mouth is soft under mine, but I can sense her surprise. She is a shy one, my Kira, and constantly surprised at my kisses, as if she is somehow not worth affection. Humans must be strange indeed if they think she is worth overlooking. “My lovely mate,” I tell her between smacking kisses as I cup her face. “How I have missed you.”

“Aehako,” she murmurs, her hands caressing mine. “You’re making a scene, love.” Her cheeks are pink—either with embarrassment or pleasure.

“Let them stare at me.” I lean in closer to her, as if sharing a secret. “I have not seen my mate in many, many nights, and my cock is the worse for it—”

Her hand covers my mouth, her cheeks even redder. Ah, that is my sweet Kira. I grin and look around. “Now where is my little Kae?”

My daughter rushes forward, arms in the air, and jumps in place in front of me, wanting to be picked up. I mock-groan as I heft her into the air. “So big now! How did you get so large while I was gone, Kae? Are you as big as Sessah now?”

She giggles, her small arms going around my neck. “No, Papa.”

“Then as big as Esha, surely,” I tease, tickling her. Even as I do, I cannot help but run my gaze over her, memorizing every bit of her appearance, looking for problems. Her soft, flat mane is the same as it ever was, her eyes bright. She looks well. I glance back at her mother, and Kira is watching us with loving exasperation. She looks well, too, though I worry that perhaps she has lost some weight. Is she pale? Does she suffer from an invisible sickness as the human Har-loh did? My heart thunders in my chest with sudden terror and I put an arm to her shoulders and pull her tight against me, holding her close and pressing a kiss to her mane. The scent of her fills my nose as I hold her close.

“Aehako? Are you all right?” Kira rubs my back lightly, then reaches down to give my tail a gentle, private stroke that makes me feel as if I am the one with pink cheeks. So bold of her. I am pleased and surprised all at once.

“I am fine,” I say, and press another kiss to her mane. “You? No sickness? You are not tired?”

“That’s a weird question to ask,” she tells me, her hand going around my waist as we head away from the group and toward our cozy hut. “Why would you think I’m sick?’

Do I say what Rokan hinted at? Or will it cause her to worry unnecessarily? I do not know what to tell her. “It is nothing,” I say after a moment’s hesitation. “Merely a hunter worrying over his mate.”

She gives me an odd look but does not question me further.

Our hut looks cozy inside, with our piles of furs stacked across from each other. I notice that while I've been gone, she's moved Kae's furs closer to our bed. When I am here, normally they are as far apart as possible to give us some privacy for matings. I wonder if there is another reason that she has moved the furs, and then chide myself for seeing problems when there are none. Still, I cannot help but move about the hut, checking the roof to ensure it is solid and that the stones surrounding the firepit are in place so no coals can escape.

"Aehako?" Kira asks again, a curious expression on her mobile human face. "What is it?"

I smile broadly at her. "It is nothing."

"Mmmhmm." She crosses her arms over her chest. "Kae, honey, why don't you give Papa a hug and then go ask Miss Stacy when the feast will be ready?"

"Feast?" I ask, curious.

"For No-Poison Day. You're back just in time."

I rub my chin, wondering if Rokan's warning was because of the human holiday. Will something bad happen during the celebration? "Eat nothing while we are not there," I caution my little daughter, tousling her mane. "Just in case."

"Just in case of what?" Kira asks.

"In case the food is bad and she catches a sickness?" I grin to take the sting out of my words, but my mate does not look amused. Even Kae looks up at me with a tiny frown on her face. She looks just like her mother when she does that. I pat my daughter's cheek. "Do as your mother says, little one. We will be along shortly."

"All right, Papa." She pauses, and hugs my leg tightly, squeezing my thigh. "I'm glad you're home."

My heart feels as if it will burst with love for this small kit. I kneel down to her height and brush her soft mane back from her little face. "You were a good girl for your mama while I was gone, were you not?"

"Always," she says happily, basking under my attention.

I nod as if this pleases me greatly. "Then you will have a good No-Poison Day. I have brought you back a special gift from the great salt lake. You can have it later."

My daughter gives me another smile and then skips out of the hut, heading toward the main part of the village.

I get to my feet again and Kira gives me a patient look, waiting. "Well?"

"I am very well," I tell her, teasing. I move forward and put my hands to her hips, pulling her body against mine. She is slimmer than a sa-khui female, my Kira, but I love the feel of her in my arms. I do not even mind that she is frowning at me. I live to turn that frown into a soft smile or a gasp of yearning. Ah, but bringing my mate to the heights of pleasure is such a delight. It has already been far too long since I have touched her, and I lean down to give her a light kiss.

My lips brush against hers and I feel a bolt of pure need surge through my body, startling in its intensity. Far too long indeed since I have touched my mate. Her mouth is soft and willing against mine, and when I intensify the kiss, she wraps her arms around my neck, pressing the length of her body against mine. "Aehako," she gasps between kisses. "Don't think you can distract me like this."

"Why not? I find it a very good distraction." I kiss her again, slicking my tongue against her smooth one, and reach through the neckline of her tunic to clasp one of her teats in my hand. The nipple is hard, thrusting against my fingers, and I groan at how fierce my need is. "I have missed you far too much, my sweet Kira."

"I missed you, too," she tells me, and then slaps a hand against my shoulder. "Wait. No distractions. What is it that's troubling you?"

I shake my head, my khui beginning a deep, steady song as I touch her. "It can wait until after I have claimed my mate."

"No," she protests, even as she lets me haul her up into my arms and carry her across our hut into our furs. "Aehako, that isn't fair—"

"Shall I show you just how unfair I can be?" I tease, pulling the laces of her tunic free until her teats are exposed to my gaze. "I made you another courting gift."

Her face flames bright pink. "You didn't."

"Oh, I did. I thought of nothing but you and Kae while I was gone. Mostly you, and your sweet, giving body. The heat of your cunt as it milks my cock. The tease of your teats as they scrape against my skin when I mount you..." I slide my hand down into her leggings, seeking her warmth. "I have had to tug my own cock far too many times during this last moon. Seems a shame when I have such a pretty mate."

She moans, arching up in the furs. "God, you are making my cootie go crazy with all that dirty talk."

"Mine is wild with need as well," I admit, a little surprised at how fierce it is this day. I have been parted from my Kira before, but never has our homecoming been so...thick with arousal. I lean in and as I do, her khui's song grows even louder. Mine changes tone, resonating harder, and then we are in perfect harmony together, our khuis loud and insistent.

And I feel it in my cock. The need in my body intensifies, so much so that it takes all the breath from my lungs.

Kira gasps, her hand pressing to her chest. "Aehako," she whispers, and her voice is so husky and lovely with need that I nearly spend as she says my name. "Is this..."

I nod slowly. "Resonance. Again."

"Oh." Her hand goes to her mouth and her eyes shimmer with tears. "I...I thought Kae would be the only one. She's such a gift, but I thought maybe that I wouldn't be able to bear more, and that I was fine with that, but...this is wonderful."

Her joy is as great as mine. I cannot smile, though. Not when Rokan's warning is still ringing in my ears...

And then I groan with the realization that I am a fool. "Rokan. That idiot."

My mate sits up, frowning at me. "Why are you talking about Rokan when we're resonating?" She grabs the front of my tunic and hauls me down against her, panting. "Shouldn't you be claiming your mate?"

Oh, I want nothing more than to sink deep inside her. I chuckle and lean in close, nuzzling her chin before claiming her lips once more. "That is what I plan on doing. I am merely laughing because Rokan insisted I be among the first to return, but he would not say why. I thought something was wrong, and have not been able to stop worrying." I shake my head. "He should have told me it was resonance."

"You know he doesn't like to point that out," she tells me, caressing my shoulder and giving me a sleepy-eyed look that makes my cock stir with excitement. "But he also shouldn't have scared you like that."

"He told me it was nothing to worry over," I admit. "But when your mate is as perfect as mine is, and your kit as clever and smart, you cannot possibly think things will get better."

"And yet," Kira says, smiling. She pauses, her smile fading away. "And yet...is this better? For you? It's going to mean changes for us. Are you happy with this?"

Happy? I am overjoyed. I touch her flat stomach. "To see you rounded with my kit? It is the best No-Poison gift ever." She flings her arms around my neck, and it takes me a moment to realize she is weeping. "Why do you cry, my mate?"

"Because you're right. This is the best No-Poison ever," she says between sobs. "And these are tears of joy."

"If you say so." I pull at her leggings. "Enough about Rokan. I will stomp on his head later for scaring me so. Now, let me see if I am making other parts of you wet with joy."

I am pleased that my mate's laughter fills our hut just moments before her cries of joy do.

# 7

**ROKAN**

My mate is not with the cluster of tribesmates who come out to greet us. I am not surprised at this. I knew that she would be in our hut when I arrived. Nor is the healer in the happy, chattering group. I smile and clasp the arms of those who crowd in, wanting to know about loved ones. I will let Vektal answer those questions, because I must be somewhere else. My Li-lah needs me.

I detangle myself from the welcomers, squeezing Vaza's shoulder in greeting as I head past him, moving toward my home. The privacy screen is up, but I can hear voices inside.

"You're home," a familiar voice exclaims before I can enter, and I see Mah-dee rushing up, her round cheeks flushed. "That's terrific, and you're just in time. I have Rollan at my house today. You can come and get him when everything's all done." At my nod, she continues. "I don't suppose Hassen came with you guys...?" There's a pleading question in her gaze.

"Not this trip," I say gently, knowing my answer will bring disappointment to my mate's sister. "We could not bring many. But there will be more trips. Your mate is well and healthy, though, and he has sent gifts for you and Masan since he could not be here."

A little sad smile touches her mouth. "Masan will be happy for that at least. I'm glad you're home for Lila. If you guys need anything, just shout. You know I'm close by."

"My thanks," I tell her, and then duck into my hut. I know the privacy screen is up, but...scratching a greeting seems foolish on my own home.

Inside, the fire is banked but the room is warm. My mate sits naked with her legs sprawled atop an old leather blanket, and Maylak, the healer, is at her side. Li-lah's long, dark mane is tangled and sweaty against her face, and she breathes hard, puffing her cheeks rapidly. Her kit-swollen belly is so large it seems distended, round and ready for our daughter to be born. She looks up as I enter, her eyes wide with surprise, and then begins to laugh.

"I held out for as long as I could," she tells me, panting and laughing all at once. Her hand goes to her stomach, which ripples in response. "But your child is determined to be born today."

I move to her side and drop to my knees, clasping her hand in mine. "I am glad I am here just in time." I brush the hair from her damp brow and lean in to kiss her.

"I'm so glad you're here," she tells me, her grip tight on my palm. "I dreamed of you last night. Do you think my khui knew? Or do you think it's the kit and she has the same ability you do?"

I have no answer for that. I always thought that my "knowing" came from my khui, but if this new kit has the same "knowing" I do and has yet to have her khui…the thought fills me with wonder.

But then Maylak murmurs something to Li-lah and my mate gets on her hands and knees, her face red with strain. I support her as best I can, though I feel helpless as she squats and bears down to birth my kit. I wish I could take the pain for her. I wish I could help with the pushing…something. Anything.

"This will be easy," the healer murmurs, and then she reaches between my Li-lah's thighs even as my mate pushes again. A moment later, Maylak is holding the deep blue, tiny body of my little daughter, her horns mere bumps on her brow, her head plastered with a wet black mane. As I watch in wonder, the healer digs a finger into the kit's mouth and cleans it out, then turns her over and gives her a gentle rub on the back.

At once, the kit begins to squall her outrage, her lungs healthy and strong.

My Li-lah bursts into tears.

"What is it?" I ask as she settles back down on her haunches. I take her hand in mine again. "What is wrong? Do you hurt?"

She shakes her head, weeping as the howling kit is put into her arms. "She sounds wonderful. So strong." And she cries anew, her face lit up with pure joy. I understand now—when our Rollan was born, my Li-lah was unable to hear. She says she did not mind most days, but she wanted to hear our son's birth. It was one reason she chose to have her hearing restored when the alien ship landed.

I lean in close and press a kiss to my mate's brow. "You did perfectly, my Li-lah."

"Shh," she whispers, caressing the little one's face as she moves the kit to her breast, offering her nipple. My mate's gaze meets mine again and she gives a little shake of her head in wonder. "It's a girl, like you said."

"I know." I smile at her. "I always know."

"Just like you knew to be here for her birth," Li-lah says, voice full of wonder.

"It is because we are one, you and I. My khui will always know when you need me," I tell my mate, and hold her close as she nurses our daughter.

# 8

**BEK**

I caress Ell-ee's back as she dozes, her body half-sprawled atop mine. She is exhausted, my mate, after our many, many rounds of mating. My hunger for her is not quite sated, but I am content to relax with her, feeling her sleeping body against mine. This is my favorite place to be, my mate pillowed against me, sharing my warmth, and her body bare for me to stroke at my leisure. I touch her arm, then trace my fingers along the delicate line of her spine, re-learning her body after so many days and nights of being apart. My Ell-ee clutches at me, even in her sleep, her hand twined in my mane as if she is afraid I will disappear and when she wakes this will all be a dream. I know this feeling, and I fight it myself. So I just keep touching her and petting her soft skin as she sleeps. It will take time. Until then, we will spend every waking moment together and every sleeping moment curled together and...

I gaze up, surprised at what I see. There is a bundle of plants hanging over the furs. As I look around the hut, I notice that there are a great many changes since I was here last. There is a sad, wilted tree in one corner, covered in garlands and with bundles of leather underneath it. Strings of colorful seeds hang between the bundles of plants, and there is a large basket near the door that looks as if it has stalks of hraku—the treat humans love so much—hanging out of it.

This is...odd.

My Ell-ee's grip tightens in my mane and she whimpers, then jerks awake, her eyes wide. She blinks for a moment and then relaxes back against me, relieved. "I dreamed you weren't there," she murmurs, caressing my chest. "I'm so glad you are."

"I will never leave you again, my mate. I mean it." I hold her close. "I am happy at your side. But...you will have to tell me why there is a dead tree in the corner of our hut."

She giggles, eyes closed as she snuggles up against me. "I was decorating."

"For the holiday?"

I can feel her nod against my chest. "I figured that if you weren't home in time, I'd just wait and we'd celebrate when you got here." Her fingers skim over my stomach. "I was making you presents, but they won't all be done."

Again, I am humbled by my mate's sweetness. "You were making gifts for me?"

"Of course." She sits up, giving me a soft smile. "You're the only person I want to spend my holiday with."

I am the luckiest male there ever was. "I brought you small things as well. Though, I did not think to bring you leaves." I gesture at the arched top of our hut. "I should have brought you some to show you that I care."

She circles my navel with a fingertip. "Just between you and me, I'm not entirely sure I understand the whole 'No-Poison' thing."

"It is in exchange for kisses. Is that not how humans do it?" I always thought it a strange custom, but humans do many strange things.

"If you wanted to kiss me, all you have to do is ask," Ell-ee murmurs. "No gifts, no leaves, no trees necessary."

"I shall kiss you every day and every night," I announce to her. "But I will still give you gifts of No-Poison. It is what we do to show we care."

"Whatever you want to do," my mate says easily, leaning down and brushing her lips against my bare chest. "Whatever you want to call it. No-Poison, Christmas...doesn't matter what it is, as long as we're together."

On that, we are very much agreed.

# 9

**LIZ**

"It's because we're pregnant, isn't it? That's why we got left behind. You don't have to lie to me. I know I'm hard to be around on my good days. I'm sure Hormonal Liz makes no friends," I tell Harlow as we sit in my tent up on the cliffs, waiting for the hunters to return for the day. Most of the hunts lately have taken a lot longer than usual because there are so many newcomers that must be brought up to speed. The island tribes are unfamiliar with snow and cold, and the human women aren't used to hunting more than a sale. As for the alien guys...I'm not convinced those red twins weren't dropped on their heads as youngsters, because they don't seem to know shit about survival. But I can't judge.

Oh wait, yes I can. That's who I am.

Harlow just gives me a sweet smile and stirs the stew over the fire. "You're just sad that you can't go with them."

"Well, yeah," I say, huffing. "Ride a dragon? That sounds cool as shit. And be home in time to celebrate No-Poison with my girls? I'd totally sign up for that. Instead, I get to stay here and babysit. Womp, womp." I make a sad trombone noise and pat my rounded stomach. "I can't even go hunting with Raahosh because of this thing. Only a jillion more months to go. Whee."

Harlow chuckles and shakes her head at me, returning to her seat. She's bigger than I am, and her movements are far more ungainly. She more or less falls backward into the stack of pillows that works as her seat, because her baby belly's so huge. At least she's put on weight now. She looks so much better than she did before. "Mine'll be any day now, hopefully." A little sigh escapes her. "I wanted Rukhar to be here, though. He's looking forward to a brother or sister so much."

"Oh, shit, don't mention the kids or I'm going to blubber like an idiot all over again." I pick up one of my bone-tipped arrows and my stone-sharpening tool, wagging it at her in warning. "No children talk." At her nod, I try to focus on my gear maintenance, but I keep thinking of my little Raashel and sweet Aayla. My girls will be getting so big. It's the first year that we're having No-Poison and Aayla's old enough to really understand what's going on. I was looking forward to seeing her big eyes light up when she saw the presents under the tree...annnd now I'm crying. "Well, shit," I say with a sniffle and wipe my nose. "That worked for all of two seconds."

"Me too," Harlow says, and sniffs as well.

It's been like this for the two days that the others have been gone. Harlow cries. I cry. Harlow cries some more. I do my best to fight off tears and then just lose it at the simplest things. I could be helping someone with firemaking, or how to add a sleeve to a tunic and boom, waterworks. Some of it's pregnancy, sure, but some of it's because I never expected to be away from my girls this long. I can't blame the newcomers. They're trying. They're really trying. But they still need help surviving. With our luck, we'd decide they can make it on their own, and then come back to a bunch of popsicles on the shore. Some of them are picking things up quickly. Samantha's smart, and Nadine's proved to be really good with hunting. Hannah knows a little about sewing and has been helping the others. The islanders are fantastic at fishing.

But some of the newcomers—like the red twins—are fucking helpless, and it's not for lack of trying. I'll never forget the look on Raahosh's face when he took them out hunting and they massacred a poor dvisti like it insulted their mom or something. They're still grasping the whole "you kill it because it's to be eaten" not "kill for funsies." Makes me wonder where the hell they came from.

Of course, that's unfair. They've been nothing but devoted to Angie, who's almost as pregnant as we are.

They're an interesting mess of a tribe, the Icehome group, but I know Raahosh feels like I do—we'd feel guilty as hell if we went home and they struggled to survive. And really, the beach is not a terrible place to be. The food is plentiful, and the brutal season is mild here compared to back home in Croatoan village. My problem is that if we stay here too much longer, we won't be home until the brutal season is over...and that means months and months without my baby girls.

And now I feel like crying all over again. I wish someone could haul them out here so we could be together.

Harlow sniffs, lost in thought, and I know she's struggling even more than I am. She's lost the ship—which she took almost as hard as Mardok did—and her Rukhar is back home safe with Gail and the others. She's finding it hard to fill her time because she's not a big hunter, and she doesn't sew much. Her thing has always been tinkering with the ship, and now that it's gone, she's got a lot of hours to fill. "Don't start bawling or you're going to make me start again," I warn her.

"I'm not crying," she says, and she's a terrible liar. "I just...feel bad for Rukh, you know?" She gives a teary giggle. "He misses Rukhar, too, but every time he tries to talk to me, I'm bawling or complaining about how much everything hurts right now." She puts her hands to her lower back and winces as she stretches. "I'm not much fun to be around."

"Yeah, me either. Raahosh hasn't gotten a blowjob in dayyyys." My poor mate.

"Liz!" Harlow chokes on her laughter. "TMI."

"What? Don't tell me you're getting all frisky with Rukh? Please, girl. This isn't my first baby. About this time, the last thing I want is for him to touch me. Add in all the emotions and I'm a fucking disaster to be around." I run my arrow along the sharpening stone and shake my head. "It's a wonder he hasn't run away screaming. But it does explain why he's been off hunting so much lately." Ever since Vektal and the others left on the dragon, I thought my mate would be spending more cuddle-time with me to comfort me. Nope. He's found every excuse he can to get the hell out of Dodge.

And I get it. I do.

Well, kind of. I'm also pissy about it, because that's who I am. But I understand. He needs the distractions.

Doesn't mean he's getting a blowjob anytime soon with that attitude, though.

But I love the guy, warts and all. He's kind of a bear sometimes, but he's my bear and I know I can be a real pain in the ass sometimes. It's why we jive so well together. We both exhaust other people, but he's never boring to me, and I suspect the same with him. After so many seasons of being mated, I still get turned on when he gives me one of those slow smiles, and his scars are as sexy as ever. Hence all the babies, I suppose. I chuckle to myself at the thought. I guess he's lucky I'm just as horny as he is.

"Hmm?" Harlow asks, looking over at me, wondering what's so funny.

I open my mouth to speak when there's a loud, off-key noise. It sounds like...well, this planet doesn't have walruses, but if it did, it'd sound like they were mating outside of my tent. I immediately forget what I'm about to say and just stare at Harlow in surprise.

"Er..." she says, and cocks her head to the side. "What was that?"

Another strange sound erupts from outside, and then I realize there are words. And a tune. Kind of.

"Dear god," I whisper to Harlow. "I think this is a song."

"Shangle bells?" she adds, voice low, and covers her mouth to muffle her horrified giggle.

It is "Jingle Bells." Kind of. A really slow, off-key version that's clearly meant to offend our ears. I get up from my seat and move to the front of the tent, pulling back the flap. Outside, Rukh and Raahosh stand, dvisti-fat candle bowls in their hands, and "sing." I try not to smile, but it's evident that my mate has no idea what the fuck he's singing, because it morphs about a third of the way through from "Jingle Bells" into "White Christmas," full of mispronunciations and wrong notes and sa-khui interpretations.

It's beyond words.

It's...the nicest thing Raahosh has ever done for me. He knows I've been sad that I'm not there for No-Poison Day with the girls. I know what he's up to, that sneaky bastard. He's trying to bring me Christmas. You can't be mated to a guy for so long without figuring out exactly how his mind works. I love it. I love that he's trying so hard. And when he tries to hit a high note—who knew there was a high note in White Christmas?—I do my best to hold back my wince.

As the "song" ends, Harlow claps her hands and gives a delighted little laugh. "Oh, that was wonderful!"

"You like?" Rukh asks, coming inside. He offers her the candle. "We learned carols for our mates."

"Obviously," I murmur, moving out of the tent as Rukh settles down next to Harlow and they kiss. She's smiling and happy and I'll let them have a moment...because I need one alone with my mate. I saunter up to Raahosh—well, as much as a heavily pregnant woman can saunter—and give him a smile. "Is this what you've been up to for the last few days? Learning Christmas carols?"

He snorts, his candle flickering. "You did not think I suddenly preferred the company of the new tribe to spending time with you?"

"This is very, very...sweet," I say, deciding to be diplomatic. "What made you decide on songs?"

"Lo-ren and Tee-ah told us it is a human tradition." He leans in, candle flickering under his chin. "There are many foolish human traditions, but I do this one for you."

Bless his heart. I slide my hand into his belt and tug him forward a step, smiling. "I'm honored that you'd put up with so many 'foolish' things just to impress me." God, even after all these seasons, just the sight of him gets me all wet between the thighs. His features are too sharp and fierce for him to be handsome in the sa-khui sense, and his childhood scars ruined any chance of that long ago, but I love his face. I love looking at him, I love that his mouth gets all tight at the edges when he smiles because his scars are pulling. I love his crooked horns. They make me crazy with need.

"My mate," he murmurs, leaning closer even as he puts the candle out with his fingertips. "I would perform no end of foolish tasks if it would make you stop crying. I cannot bring the girls here with us, but I promise I will try to make our time together enjoyable."

"You nut," I whisper, getting all stupidly emotional again. "Every day with you is a good day. The girls are safe. That's all that matters. I'm just being silly and emotional, but I appreciate your effort."

"I have learned another carol," he admits. "Do you want to hear it?"

"Fuck no." I tug on his belt again. "I'd rather find someplace quiet and give you a present."

"A present?" He looks surprised. "For me?"

I nod slowly. "It's hot and wet and loves to suck on hard things." I lean in and whisper. "Spoiler: it's my mouth."

"I think I like this holiday," he tells me.

"Thought you might." I grin and pull on his belt again, tugging him forward. "Now let's go take over the supply tent before someone notices we're missing."

His eyes gleam with anticipation, and for the first time in days, I feel lighter.

Happy.

# 10

**VEKTAL**

My Georgie cannot stop kissing me. It does not matter that others crowd around us, eager to greet, or that Vuh-ron-ca and Ash-tar trail behind me like lost kits. It does not matter to her that I am so much taller that I must stoop over so she can kiss my face over and over again. She just presses her mouth to mine over and over again with delight. "You're home," she says. "I'm so glad!"

I chuckle as she plants another kiss on my mouth. "Let me take a look at you, my mate."

"In a minute," she tells me, and then kisses me again, this time teasing my lips with her tongue. Ah, she is playful this day, my mate. Hopefully this means the new kit she carries in her belly has settled more.

I wait, patient, as she kisses me once more and then releases me. I straighten and take her hands in mine, stepping backward and studying my beaming mate with a critical eye. When I left, she was thin, her belly flat in the early days of her carrying. She is slightly rounded now, her color better, and her cheeks are plump. "You are well, my sweet resonance?"

"Never better," Georgie tells me, and puts a hand to her gently swelling stomach. "Right after you left, it was like he decided that he was fine with everything. No more puking. Now I'm just hungry all the time." She sighs, but it is a happy one. "I hope you don't mind your mate fattening up."

"I can think of nothing better," I tell her, pleased. I clasp her hand tightly in mine and then glance around. "My girls...?"

"Hiding." She grimaces. "We didn't know if it was safe. They're in the longhouse. Someone said they saw a big monster in the skies, and then it was chaos. I didn't realize it was you guys—"

"The monster is truth," I admit, and then pull my mate against my shoulder, tucking her under my arm before she can ask more questions. I gesture at Vuh-ron-ca and Ash-tar, who stand behind us. "These are two of the newcomers. One of them can become a monster."

"A dragon," Vuh-ron-ca corrects me, and then her cheeks flush as she looks at her mate.

"A drakoni," Ash-tar corrects his mate, grinning. "But I like 'monster.' It sounds fearsome."

My Georgie puts a hand to her mouth. "Oh! I didn't realize you'd brought newcomers. I was so focused on looking for you." She pushes out of my grip, giving my stomach a gentle pat before she turns into "chief's wife." "Welcome! I'm Georgie, Vektal's mate. Were there only two of you in the spaceship?"

"Oh no," Vuh-ron-ca says with a smile, even as she extends her hand to my mate. "There were twenty all right. And there are a bunch of islanders, too."

My mate turns back to me, a bewildered look on her face. "Islanders?"

"It is a very long story, my sweet resonance," I tell her. I am proud of how quickly she approaches the others, ready to make them comfortable and at home with us. She is the perfect mate for a chief. I watch her as she greets them both, and my gaze slides to the soft curve of her bottom. It is plumper than before, and I approve of this. I approve of this very much. Just the sight of her tailless bottom makes my cock remember how long it has been since I have claimed my mate.

Ah, but it is good to be home.

"Papa," a familiar little voice cries out, and my heart thumps with pure joy.

I turn, and racing out from the longhouse is my oldest daughter, Talie. She holds little Vekka's hand, letting her younger sister toddle alongside her as fast as she can. In fact, she races so fast that I am sure Vekka is going to fall forward, so I rush to meet them, and manage to scoop up both daughters just in time. "My girls," I call out, and I cannot stop grinning. "Look at you!"

"Yes, look at you both, disobeying your mother," Georgie calls out, exasperated, but I hear the laughter in her voice.

I kiss both of them over and over, alternating kisses between the two of them, much like how Georgie kissed me so many times. I have missed these little ones as much as I missed my sweet resonance. "Have you been good?" I ask as Talie gives me a smacking kiss and Vekka gives me a wet press of her mouth to my cheek. "Listened to your mama?"

"Most of the time," my Talie says, sounding so adult. "You aren't going to go away again, are you, Papa?"

Such a difficult question to answer. "Not this night," I assure them both, and turn to my mate, my arms full of my kits. My heart is so full of joy in this moment that I cannot stop smiling. Being chief is good. Helping the others in their journey to survive, that is good. But being Papa and mate?

That is best of all.

Georgie ushers Vuh-ron-ca and Ash-tar forward. "I have a million questions for everyone. Just promise me that everyone that's not here is well and I'll be able to relax."

I glance out at the rest of the tribe that has gathered around. There are anxious mothers, anxious sons, worried parents. I feel guilty that there was not enough room on Ash-tar's back to bring all home. "Everyone is quite healthy," I reassure them. "We could not fit all on Ash-tar's back, but there will be more trips to the Icehome camp and more returning home as quickly as possible."

"But everyone's safe?" Stay-see steps forward, asking. At her side, she cradles an arm around Air-ee-aw-nuh, who is deathly pale and trembling.

"They are all well," I reassure them. "And they have sent gifts since they could not be here tonight. Especially Zolaya."

Air-ee-aw-nuh gives me a timid smile and squeezes Stay-see's hand, some of the color returning to her face. "Thank God."

"Well, if there are stories to be told, I want to hear them," Georgie declares, moving forward and gesturing at the longhouse. "We were all just about to enjoy our No-Poison feast before you got here. Now we have all new stories to hear over dinner. Come on, then!"

"No-Poison?" I hear Vuh-ron-ca ask.

"Long story," Georgie tells her, pulling her forward. "Vektal, will you bring the girls?" My mate looks over at me.

I nod, hefting them onto my shoulders. "Hold on to Papa's horns," I say to my daughters. "And tell me if you were good while I was gone."

"Very good," Talie says, all confidence. "Mama says I am getting a special No-Poison gift tonight." She pats my forehead. "I think it was you, wasn't it, Papa?"

And I feel as if my heart has melted in my chest. "Maybe it was." I glance over at my beautiful mate, and she is looking over at me, her eyes soft with love. She heard that, too, it seems.

Ah, but it is good to be home.

“But what of the others?” The female known as Shail steps forward. She is Vaza’s pleasure-mate, and she has little Rukhar at her side. He holds her hand tightly. “What of Rukh and Harlow? Liz and Raahosh? Don’t they want to come home and see their babies?”

Ah. I nod at her. “They do, but there was no room this time. With Ash-tar’s permission, once he and his mate have spent a few days with the healer, they will return to the Icehome village. The kits may go with them. There is no danger there.”

Rukhar’s young face lights up in a smile.

“If it’s not dangerous,” Gail says, but she does not sound certain.

“It is not,” I reassure her. “There is already one kit there.”

“A kit?” my mate asks, surprised. “Whose?”

“The islanders brought with them an orphaned kit. No more than a few turns of the moons old. They feed him eggs and take turns watching him."

"Islanders?" my mate exclaims.

"Eggs?" Shail retorts, aghast. "Oh hell, no. Someone needs to step up and parent that baby." She points at herself. "And I know just the woman." She gives Rukhar's hand a little shake. "Looks like you're gonna have company heading back to that beach, little man."

This is a good thing. Shail is very good with kits, and Vaza will go with her. He is experienced with hunting and fishing, and another set of hands will be useful. "Leezh and Raahosh will want their girls with them, as well."

"We can bring the children," Shail assures me.

"Are there many females?" Sessah asks, stepping forward. His eyes are bright with interest.

"Many," I assure him, and I suspect I have found yet another volunteer to visit the Icehome tribe.

This is all perfect. Kits will be reunited with family, and newcomers will welcome the help of those at ease with our land. And I...I will get to stay home with my mate and kits and know that my tribes—both of them—are doing well.

I cast a look over at my Georgie, and I see she is giving me a look of promise that suggests many, many things when we are alone again.

Ah yes. It is *very* good to be home.

# 11

**ELLY**

espite my best efforts to look as if I'm still asleep, my stomach rumbles.

Bek rubs my butt. "I know you are awake." His voice is soft and I can feel his tail still twined around my knee. My body's spooned against his and I'm in no particular hurry to move. "We should join the others in the celebration. They will be looking for us."

I half-groan and hide my face under the furs. I don't want to move from this spot. "I'm fine. Let's just stay here."

Bek leans in and nibbles on my shoulder. "If nothing else, let us go eat."

I wait for him to comment on how thin I am, or point out that I haven't been eating like I should, but when I hear his stomach rumble, I feel guilty. Maybe he's the hungry one. "All right, but promise we won't stay long. I want tonight to be about us." And the next day, and the next day, and the next day...I'm greedy like that.

"It will be," Bek promises me. "We will come back to our hut and roll back the smoke-flap so we can look at the stars together."

Oh. I love doing that with him. It's been far too long. Pleased, I turn and give him a fierce kiss before rising out of bed to get dressed. The nights are getting colder, which means that bundling up in all my fur wraps is a job all on its own. I'm busy concentrating on putting on my layers when I notice Bek is at my side, a leather-wrapped bundle in his hands.

Wordless, he holds it out to me.

I look up at him in surprise. "What...?"

"Your No-Poison gifts. I have not collected leaves for you, but I can do so tomorrow." He nudges the package toward me. "Please. Take it."

I do, and it feels lumpy and heavy all at once. I blink up at him, still astonished. "You made me presents?"

He nods, his expression a little stern, as if he's uncomfortable...or shy. "I could think of nothing else but my mate while we were separated. Every rock made me think of something new to show you, every bird in the sky something we were not sharing together. So I collected you things so we could share them when I returned."

My eyes blur with tears. I carefully set the present down on our bed and then fling my arms around his waist, burying my face against his chest. "I love it."

With a chuckle, Bek rubs my back. "You have not even looked at what I have given you yet."

I don't need to. His words have been the best gift I've ever been given. Even if it's a bag full of sand, I'll adore it because of the thought behind it. I squeeze him tightly, so full of love for him that I could burst.

We sit down on the furs, facing each other, and I unwrap my package with reverence. There, laid out in front of me, are mementos from his travels. He explains each one as I pick through them. There's a pretty stone from the walk there, a tiny, shiny component stolen from the alien ship. There's a bag of salt from the ocean, and since I know how treasured spices are around here, this is a huge gift on its own. There are tiny, spiny things that have dried into the shapes of wiggly, spiralized stars. And there's a bag of shells. The shells are similar to the ones on earth—pearly, swirly, ridged—but still alien enough for me to gasp over their shapes and wonder at the creatures that filled them. Each shell has a small set of holes drilled through it, and I hold one up to Bek, a question in my eyes.

"Ah. Yes." He touches the one I hold in my palm, his fingers skating over my skin. "I wanted to make you a necklace. Something pretty to wear. But then I remembered the collars...and I did not think you would like it. So I drilled holes in them that you may sew them to a tunic and admire them that way."

I blink rapidly, because I'm going to start crying. It's the most thoughtful gift I could imagine. He remembers what I like and dislike. He remembers me when he walks on the shores. More than that, I imagine him sitting by the fire each night, carefully drilling holes in the tiny, delicate shells so he can gift them to me.

And now I can make myself a tunic that shows everyone just how much Bek loves me. "It's wonderful."

The smile that lights his face is the warmest, most beautiful thing I have ever seen. Tonight, I feel like the luckiest girl in the world.

In several worlds, actually.

## ALSO THIS MONTH - FROM THE CLUB!

Need your holiday fix? Kati Wilde, Alexa Riley, and Ella Goode are also writing Christmas stories! Watch for the following to be released over the next few days!

*HOME FOR CHRISTMAS*

by Alexa Riley

*THE LAST CHRISTMAS PRESENT*
by Ella Goode

*ALL HE WANTS FOR CHRISTMAS*
by Kati Wilde

# CAST OF CHARACTERS

*At Croatoan*

**Mated Couples and their kits**

---

Vektal (Vehk-tall) – The chief of the sa-khui. Mated to Georgie.

Georgie – Human woman (and unofficial leader of the human females). Has taken on a dual-leadership role with her mate. Currently pregnant with her third kit.

Talie (Tah-lee) – Their first daughter.

Vekka (Veh-kah) – Their second daughter.

---

Maylak (May-lack) – Tribe healer. Mated to Kashrem.

Kashrem (Cash-rehm) - Her mate, also a leather-worker.

Esha (Esh-uh) – Their teenage daughter.

Makash (Muh-cash) — Their younger son.

---

Sevvah (Sev-uh) – Tribe elder, mother to Aehako, Rokan, and Sessah

Oshen (Aw-shen) – Tribe elder, her mate

Sessah (Ses-uh) - Their youngest son

---

Ereven (Air-uh-ven) Hunter, mated to Claire. Currently at Icehome beach.

Claire – Mated to Ereven

Erevair (Air-uh-vair) - Their first child, a son

Relvi (Rell-vee) – Their second child, a daughter

---

Liz – Raahosh's mate and huntress. Currently at Icehome beach.

Raahosh (Rah-hosh) – Her mate. A hunter and brother to Rukh. Currently at Icehome beach.

Raashel (Rah-shel) – Their daughter.

Aayla (Ay-lah) – Their second daughter

---

Stacy – Mated to Pashov. Unofficial tribe cook.

Pashov (Pah-showv) – son of Kemli and Borran, brother to Farli, Zennek, and Salukh. Mate of Stacy. Currently at Icehome beach.

Pacy (Pay-see) – Their first son.

Tash (Tash) – Their second son.

---

Nora – Mate to Dagesh. Currently pregnant after a second resonance.

Dagesh (Dah-zhesh) (the g sound is swallowed) – Her mate. A hunter.

Anna & Elsa – Their twin daughters.

---

Harlow – Mate to Rukh. Once 'mechanic' to the Elders' Cave. Currently pregnant after a second resonance. Currently at Icehome beach.

Rukh (Rookh) – Former exile and loner. Original name Maarukh. (Mah-rookh). Brother to Raahosh. Mate to Harlow. Father to Rukhar. Currently at Icehome beach.

Rukhar (Roo-car) – Their son.

---

Megan – Mate to Cashol. Mother to Holvek.

Cashol (Cash-awl) – Mate to Megan. Hunter. Father to Holvek.

Currently at Icehome beach.

Holvek (Haul-vehk) – their son.

---

Marlene (Mar-lenn) – Human mate to Zennek. French.

Zennek (Zehn-eck) – Mate to Marlene. Father to Zalene. Brother to Pashov, Salukh, and Farli. Currently at Icehome beach.

Zalene (Zah-lenn) – daughter to Marlene and Zennek.

---

Ariana – Human female. Mate to Zolaya. Currently pregnant. Basic school 'teacher' to tribal kits.

Zolaya (Zoh-lay-uh) – Hunter and mate to Ariana. Father to Analay. Currently at Icehome beach.

Analay (Ah-nuh-lay) – Their son.

---

Tiffany – Human female. Mated to Salukh. Tribal botanist.

Salukh (Sah-luke) – Hunter. Son of Kemli and Borran, brother to Farli, Zennek, and Pashov. Currently at Icehome beach.

Lukti (Lookh-tee) – Their son.

---

Aehako (Eye-ha-koh) –Mate to Kira, father to Kae. Son of Sevvah and Oshen, brother to Rokan and Sessah.

Kira – Human woman, mate to Aehako, mother of Kae. Was the first to be abducted by aliens and wore an ear-translator for a long time.

Kae (Ki –rhymes with 'fly') – Their daughter.

---

Kemli (Kemm-lee) – Female elder, mother to Salukh, Pashov, Zennek, and Farli. Tribe herbalist.

Borran (Bore-awn) – Her mate, elder. Tribe brewer.

---

Josie – Human woman. Mated to Haeden. Currently pregnant for a third time.

Haeden (Hi-den) – Hunter. Previously resonated to Zalah, but she died (along with his khui) in the khui-sickness before resonance could be completed. Now mated to Josie.

Joden (Joe-den) – Their first child, a son.

Joha (Joe-hah) – Their second child, a daughter.

---

Rokan (Row-can) – Oldest son to Sevvah and Oshen. Brother to Aehako and Sessah. Adult male hunter. Now mated to Lila. Has 'sixth' sense.

Lila – Maddie's sister. Once hearing impaired, recently reacquired on *The Tranquil Lady* via med bay. Resonated to Rokan. Currently pregnant for a second time.

Rollan (Row-lun) – Their first child, a son.

---

Hassen (Hass-en) – Hunter. Previously exiled. Mated to Maddie. Currently at Icehome beach.

Maddie – Lila's sister. Found in second crash. Mated to Hassen.

Masan (Mah-senn) – Their son.

---

Asha (Ah-shuh) – Mate to Hemalo. Mother to Hashala (deceased) and Shema.

Hemalo (Hee-muh-low) – Mate to Asha. Father to Hashala (deceased) and Shema.

Shema (Shee-muh) – Their daughter.

---

Farli – (Far-lee) Adult daughter to Kemli and Borran. Her brothers are Salukh, Zennek, and Pashov. She has a pet dvisti named Chompy (Chahm-pee). Mated to Mardok. Pregnant. Currently at Icehome beach.

Mardok (Marr-dock) – Bron Mardok Vendasi, from the planet Ubeduc VII. Arrived on *The Tranquil Lady*. Mechanic and ex-soldier. Resonated to Farli and elected to stay behind with the tribe. Currently at Icehome beach.

---

Bek – (Behk) – Hunter. Brother to Maylak. Mated to Elly.

Elly – Former human slave. Kidnapped at a very young age and has spent much of life in a cage or enslaved. First to resonate amongst the former slaves brought to Not-Hoth. Mated to Bek. Pregnant.

---

Harrec (Hair-ek) – Hunter. Squeamish. Also a tease. Recently resonated to Kate.

Kate – Human female. Extremely tall & strong, with white-blonde curly hair. Recently resonated to Harrec. Pregnant.

---

Warrek (War-ehk) – Tribal hunter and teacher. Son to Eklan (now deceased). Resonated to Summer.

Summer – Human female. Tends to ramble in speech when nervous. Chess aficionado. Recently resonated to Warrek.

---

Taushen (Tow – rhymes with cow – shen) – Hunter. Recently mated to Brooke. Experiencing a happiness renaissance. Currently at Icehome beach.

Brooke – Human female with fading pink hair. Former hairdresser, fond of braiding the hair of anyone that walks close enough. Mated to Taushen and recently pregnant. Currently at

Icehome beach.

**Unmated Elders**

---

Drayan (Dry-ann) – Elder.

Drenol (Dree-nowl) – Elder.

Vadren (Vaw-dren) – Elder.

Vaza (Vaw-zhuh) – Widower and elder. Loves to creep on the ladies. Currently flirting with Gail.

---

Gail – Divorced older human woman. Had a son back on Earth (deceased). Approx fiftyish in age. Allows Vaza to creep on her (she likes the attention). From the batch of 'Bek Rescues'.

*At Icehome*

Lauren – Pod girl. Went missing when the ship went down. Mated to K'thar.

K'thar – Sakh male, member of the island tribe. Mated to Lauren.

Ashtar – Golden-skinned male slave of drakoni race, resonated to Veronica upon receiving khui.

Veronica – Clumsy human female who resonated to Ashtar upon receiving khui.

Tia – Youngest of pod girls.

## ICE PLANET BARBARIANS READING LIST

Are you all caught up on Ice Planet Barbarians? Need a refresher? Click through to borrow or buy!

Ice Planet Barbarians – Georgie's Story
Barbarian Alien – Liz's Story
Barbarian Lover – Kira's Story
Barbarian Mine – Harlow's Story
Ice Planet Holiday – Claire's Story (novella)
Barbarian's Prize – Tiffany's Story
Barbarian's Mate – Josie's Story
Having the Barbarian's Baby – Megan's Story (short story)
Ice Ice Babies – Nora's Story (short story)
Barbarian's Touch – Lila's Story
Calm - Maylak's Story (short story)
Barbarian's Taming – Maddie's Story
Aftershocks (short story)
Barbarian's Heart – Stacy's Story
Barbarian's Hope – Asha's Story
Barbarian's Choice – Farli's Story

## WANT MORE?

For more information about upcoming books in the Ice Planet Barbarians, Fireblood Dragons, or any other books by Ruby Dixon, like me on Facebook or subscribe to my new release newsletter. I love sharing snippets of books in progress and fan art! Come join the fun.

As always - thanks for reading!

<3 Ruby

PS - Want to discuss my books without me staring over your shoulder? There's a group for that, too! Ruby Dixon - Blue Barbarian Babes (over on Facebook) has all of your barbarian and dragon needs. :) Enjoy!

Printed in Great Britain
by Amazon